ENEMY INFILTRATION

———

CAROL ERICSON

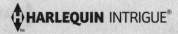

If you purchased this book without a cover you should be aware that this book is stolen property. It was reported as "unsold and destroyed" to the publisher, and neither the author nor the publisher has received any payment for this "stripped book."

Recycling programs
for this product may
not exist in your area.

ISBN-13: 978-1-335-60469-9

Enemy Infiltration

Copyright © 2019 by Carol Ericson

All rights reserved. Except for use in any review, the reproduction or utilization of this work in whole or in part in any form by any electronic, mechanical or other means, now known or hereafter invented, including xerography, photocopying and recording, or in any information storage or retrieval system, is forbidden without the written permission of the publisher, Harlequin Enterprises Limited, 22 Adelaide St. West, 40th Floor, Toronto, Ontario M5H 4E3, Canada.

This is a work of fiction. Names, characters, places and incidents are either the product of the author's imagination or are used fictitiously, and any resemblance to actual persons, living or dead, business establishments, events or locales is entirely coincidental.

This edition published by arrangement with Harlequin Books S.A.

For questions and comments about the quality of this book, please contact us at CustomerService@Harlequin.com.

® and TM are trademarks of Harlequin Enterprises Limited or its corporate affiliates. Trademarks indicated with ® are registered in the United States Patent and Trademark Office, the Canadian Intellectual Property Office and in other countries.

Printed in U.S.A.

"Whatever you do, don't give in."

"Come here."

He stroked her hair, and then he took her by the shoulders and gently pushed her away, looking into her face.

She blinked as if emerging from a sweet, sweet dream. "What was that for?"

"You looked like you needed a hug, and I know I sure as hell did."

"Any time, Tex." Tilting her head, she touched her cheek to the back of his hand. "You ready to enter the lion's den now?"

"As long as you stick by my side."

"You've been by mine all this time. Where else would I be?"

His thumbs inched up the sides of her neck until he wedged one beneath her chin. He slanted his mouth across hers and caressed her lips with his.

When he drew away, he brushed his thumb against her throbbing lower lip. "Do I have to apologize for that?"

R0455900194

Carol Ericson is a bestselling, award-winning author of more than forty books. She has an eerie fascination for true-crime stories, a love of film noir and a weakness for reality TV, all of which fuel her imagination to create her own tales of murder, mayhem and mystery. To find out more about Carol and her current projects, please visit her website at www.carolericson.com, "where romance flirts with danger."

Books by Carol Ericson

Harlequin Intrigue

Her Alibi

Red, White and Built: Delta Force Deliverance

Enemy Infiltration

Red, White and Built: Pumped Up

Delta Force Defender
Delta Force Daddy
Delta Force Die Hard

Red, White and Built

Locked, Loaded and SEALed
Alpha Bravo SEAL
Bullseye: SEAL
Point Blank SEAL
Secured by the SEAL
Bulletproof SEAL

Target: Timberline

Single Father Sheriff
Sudden Second Chance
Army Ranger Redemption
In the Arms of the Enemy

Brothers in Arms: Retribution

Under Fire
The Pregnancy Plot
Navy SEAL Spy
Secret Agent Santa

Harlequin Intrigue Noir

Toxic

Visit the Author Profile page at Harlequin.com.

CAST OF CHARACTERS

Lana Moreno—The unusual circumstances surrounding the death of her brother prompt this headstrong horse trainer to push for answers, but somebody is pushing back and Lana is forced to seek protection from the one man who may hold the key to her brother's murder.

Logan Hess—Determined to clear his Delta Force commander's name, Logan seeks out the sister of a marine killed at an embassy outpost and discovers she's in possession of information that has endangered her. Now his desire to protect Lana is as great as his duty to exonerate his commander.

Gilbert Moreno—This marine was killed while guarding an embassy outpost, but before he died, he kept a journal detailing strange events at the embassy.

Drew Halliday—The new ranch hand at Logan's family's ranch attracts the attention of Logan's sister, but the timing of his arrival might be more than a coincidence.

Alexa Hess—Logan's younger sister is a wild child, but will her high spirits jeopardize Logan's investigation and put Lana in harm's way?

Maj Rex Denver—Framed for working with a terrorist group, the Delta Force commander has gone AWOL and is on the run, but he knows he can count on his squad to have his back and help clear his name.

Prologue

He grabbed the barrel of the old Kalashnikov as he took his place around the fire and yanked it away from him and toward the wall of the hut. "How do you expect me to think with that in my face?"

Rafi, the leader of the group, kicked at a mound of dirt in front of the man hoisting the rifle. "No need for that, Mateen. We've taken Major Denver's weapons from him."

"He's Delta Force." Mateen spit into the dirt. "He could use your shoe as a weapon and you wouldn't even know it was off your foot."

The other men around the circle laughed and Denver chuckled along with them. Good to know Delta Force still struck fear in the hearts of enemies and frenemies alike, and Mateen wasn't too far off the mark with his comment.

Denver crossed his legs beneath him and stretched out his hands to the crackling fire. He winked at Massoud, the boy who'd brought him down from the mountain, now crouched behind his father, Rafi.

Massoud offered a shy smile in return, his tough-guy bravado no longer necessary in the company of men.

One of the men began handing around earthenware bowls of lamb stew, which Massoud's mother had been cooking when they'd barged in on her. Denver hadn't seen the woman since.

He passed two bowls along the circle and claimed the third for his own, cupping his hands around smooth clay to warm them more than anything else. Then he tore off a piece of the flatbread making the rounds and plunged it into the steaming concoction, chock-full of chunks of lamb meat and vegetables.

He blew on the bread, dripping gravy, and then shoved it into his mouth, burning his tongue, anyway. He didn't care. The warmth and spices in the stew made his nose run, and he didn't care about that, either.

The other men must've been as hungry as he was. For several minutes, the only sounds from the hut with the dirt floor were slurping and chomping as the men gnawed the tough meat with their teeth and sopped up the gravy with the bread.

When he finished, Denver wiped his mouth with the back of his hand and screwed the bowl into the dirt. "Now, tell me everything you know about Pazir and how our meeting was compromised."

Rafi raised his finger and then snapped. Massoud scurried around the circle, collecting all the bowls. He retreated to a corner and soaked up the dregs of everyone's stew with the leftover bread he'd snatched from the fire.

A pang of guilt shot through Denver's now-full stomach. Massoud's mother hadn't cooked enough stew for an unexpected gathering like this. The men had eaten Massoud's dinner and probably his mother's, as well.

Rafi folded his hands against his belly. "Pazir was foolish, a talker."

The other men nodded and grunted.

"He told someone about our meeting?"

"He told many someones." Rafi waved his hand, encompassing the men sitting at the fire. "We all knew about it."

"Is Pazir still alive?" Denver massaged his temple with two fingers, the smoke in the hut giving him a headache.

"We don't know." Rafi shrugged. "When he found out what happened at the meeting place—an Army Ranger killed, one of your Delta Force team members going over the side of a cliff and you taking off—he disappeared."

"He could be dead." Denver drew a cross in the dirt and then wiped it out with his fist.

"No body." One of the other men spoke up. "Al Tariq likes to send messages. No body, no message."

"If it was Al Tariq who disrupted the meeting. And my Delta Force teammate? Did you hear anything about him?" Denver held his breath. He'd tried to save Asher Knight by pushing him out of the way. His action had spared Knight the bullet, but he'd tumbled over the cliff's edge instead.

"Don't know." Rafi shook his head. "Didn't hear."

Denver blew out a breath. The others had heard about the death of the Army Ranger, but not Asher. Maybe that meant he'd made it. "I need to get another meeting with Pazir. Can any of you facilitate that?"

The men exchanged glances around the circle.

One of the men coughed and swirled his hot tea in his cup. "That could be dangerous."

Another of the men jumped up and tossed the contents of his cup into the fire, which snapped and sizzled. "*He's* dangerous. He shouldn't be here. You should've killed him on the mountainside, Massoud."

"Enough." Rafi sliced a hand through the air. "Major Denver is the enemy of our enemy. That is enough. Al Tariq has been inciting trouble and violence in the region for over a year now and doing it with secret international support. If Major Denver wants to end that, it's good enough for me. It should be good enough for all of us."

A quiet man seated next to Rafi, who hadn't said a word all night, stood up. "I know someone who can reach Pazir. The man has been working as a driver and translator like Pazir had been, and he might know where he is. He can let him know you survived and want to talk to him."

"I appreciate that." Denver bowed his head. "I appreciate all of it."

Later that night after more tea and a shared hookah, Rafi allowed Denver to bunk down by the fire.

With the rest of the inhabitants asleep in the hut, Denver rolled toward the fire and then away. He stretched out his legs and then brought his knees to his chest.

The smoke had his head pounding again—or maybe it was the spicy lamb stew. He sat up and drew the rough blanket around his shoulders. Then he crept to the doorway of the hut.

He slipped outside to inhale the cold, fresh air. His head jerked as a glimmer of light from the rocks at the bottom of the foothills caught his attention.

He squinted into the darkness and saw a second point of light bobbing next to the first. He grabbed his weapon by the door, hoisted it and peered through the night scope.

Uttering a curse, he tracked the guns bearing down on the village. He'd brought the enemy to their doorstep… Now nobody was safe.

Chapter One

Lana's brown cowboy boots clumped over the wood floor of her congressman's office building. As furtive glances followed her, she tipped back her head, nose in the air and took even heavier steps—the louder the better. She wanted to create a stir.

"Miss, excuse me." The blonde at the front desk half rose from her chair, phone at her ear. "Miss, you can't go in there."

Lana spun around, one hand jiggling the locked doorknob, the other on her hip. "Because it's locked or because I'm not welcome? I'm a taxpaying constituent."

"I'm sure you are, but Congressman Cordova is in a meeting right now." The assistant waved her manicured fingers at a pathetic suggestion box stuck to the wall. "You're welcome to leave a note."

"I've left notes. I've left voice mails. I've left emails." Lana leveled a finger at the blond gatekeeper. "I'm pretty sure I've spoken to you on a number of occasions, and Congressman Cordova—" the name rolled off Lana's tongue in a perfect Spanish accent "—has yet to return my notes, voice mails or emails.

Excuse me if I have a hard time believing he's going to check his suggestion box. I have a suggestion. Tell him to open this damned door and meet with one of his constituents."

The assistant plopped back down in her chair, swiveled away from Lana and whispered into the phone. She put down the receiver and cleared her throat. "If you'd like to leave your name and number, the congressman will call when he's free."

"When will that be? Never?" Lana twisted the doorknob and kicked the door with the toe of her boot. "Open the door, or you'll be sorry, Cordova."

The woman at the desk grabbed the phone again and held up the receiver, shaking it at Lana. "Miss, if you don't leave at once, I'm calling security."

"Do it." Lana leaned against the impenetrable door and folded her arms across her chest. "This will play well."

The blonde's cool exterior and her voice finally cracked as she shouted into the phone, "Someone needs to get over here, right away."

Before the final word left her lips, two security guards charged through the side door of the building. Cordova's office only gave the illusion of his approachability. Barriers and layers protected him from the common people just as surely as they had protected a czar from his serfs.

As the two goons veered in her direction, Lana thrust out her hands. "I'm not going anywhere until I talk to my congressman. I pay his salary—yours, too."

"Ma'am." The bigger security guard spread out his

hands, which looked like slabs of pink beef. "Go about this the right way. Don't cause any trouble today."

"Trouble?" Lana sniffed and blinked her eyes rapidly. She refused to give in to tears here. Did she have any left? "You ain't seen nothin' yet."

The big guy rolled his eyes at his slightly smaller partner and said, "Are you even five feet tall? You're not going to put up a fight, are you, ma'am?"

Lana widened her stance, the heels of her boots digging into the polished floor. "Five foot two."

Security guard number two snorted. "Ma'am, you're going to have to leave the premises, one way or another."

"How about *you* leave the premises, and I meet with my congressman."

"I—I can make an appointment for you with Congressman Cordova." Cordova's assistant swung her chair in front of her computer, her hands poised over the keyboard. "He's free tomorrow at three o'clock. Will that work for you?"

"Hmm." Lana tapped a finger against her chin as she tilted her head to the side. "No. Right now works for me."

The taller, bigger, beefier security guard took a step forward. "Ma'am, this isn't working for anyone right now. You're going to have to leave and make an appointment through Tessa later."

"I don't want to leave, and Cordova is never going to keep an appointment with *me*. I'm on his no-call list." Lana ground her back teeth together.

Tessa's face blanched, almost matching the color

of her hair. As the security duo moved forward with purpose, Tessa shouted, "Wait!"

But the guards had both started speaking at once in coaxing tones as they moved in on Lana, drowning out Tessa's exclamation.

They each took one of Lana's arms and peeled her off the congressman's door. They started to march her toward the front entrance, the one facing the sidewalk, the one facing the public.

Tessa had jumped from her seat, the chair banging against the wall behind her. "What's your name? What's your name?"

Lana cranked her head over her shoulder and smiled at Tessa, her pale face now crumpled with worry. "Lana. Lana Moreno."

"Wait…don't." Tessa scurried around the desk, banging her hip on the corner.

The security guards had embraced their mission and continued propelling Lana to the exit—flipping the congressman from the frying pan into the fire.

The three of them burst through the double doors into the wintry Greenvale sun, straight into the arms of the media Lana had called earlier.

Cameras zoomed in and microphones materialized out of thin air.

"Did Congressman Cordova kick you out of his office, Lana?"

"Did he have any answers for you?"

"Do you think this shows his disdain for the military?"

Both of the security guards dropped her arms so

fast and at the same time, she listed to the side. The shorter guy growled. "What the hell is this?"

"It's a news conference, which never would've happened had Cordova agreed to meet with me."

She brushed off the sleeves of her brown suede jacket, tugged on its lapels and stepped in front of a microphone. "Yes, Congressman Luis Cordova refused to meet with me, and he's refused to answer any of my emails. You can make your own determination whether or not that shows disrespect for our military as he continues to cover up the circumstances behind the deaths of three marines in Nigeria."

"Ms. Moreno." The congressman magically appeared in the doorway behind her, his unctuous tone, as smooth as oil, swirling through the chaos on the sidewalk. "I was just finishing up with my meeting when I heard the commotion. I told my assistant to clear all my calls immediately. Come back into my office with me. I apologize for the misunderstanding."

Lana nodded, backed away from the mic and swept past the two security guards, now trying to keep the reporters from following her and the congressman.

Five minutes later, ensconced in a deep leather chair across from Congressman Cordova, a glass of water in front of her, Lana took a deep breath. "I'm sorry I had to resort to those means, but you wouldn't acknowledge any of my communications."

Cordova swept a hand over the top of his head, slicking his salt-and-pepper hair back from his forehead. "You saw the report, Ms. Moreno. There's no mystery, no cover-up. Your brother and the other marines were attacked outside the embassy outpost by a band of marauding criminals. Nigeria can be a lawless place, especially away from the big cities."

"Really?" She crossed one leg over the other and took a sip of water. "What was the U.S. Government doing in that particular area of Nigeria?"

"That is classified information. Your brother didn't even know what they were doing there."

"I wouldn't be so sure of that." She drummed her fingers on his desk. "I'm waiting for the Marine Corps to ship his belongings to me. They could even arrive as early as this afternoon. Gil always kept a journal. I can't wait to read what he wrote in that journal."

"I'm sure it will be a great comfort to you, Ms. Moreno. *Lo siento por su perdida*." He steepled his fingers and bowed his head.

Tears stung her nose. "I don't need you to be sorry for my loss. I need you to use your position on the House Foreign Affairs Committee to open up an investigation of what went down at that embassy outpost— a real investigation."

"The Committee has no reason to believe anything other than the initial report, a report I went out of my way to send you, by the way."

Uncrossing her legs, she hunched forward, the ends of her long hair sweeping the glossy surface of his desk. "A report so heavily redacted, I could barely read it through the black lines."

"A necessity, but I'm sure you got the gist of the information. A marauding band of…"

"Criminals." She smacked her fist on the desk, causing the pens in the holder to dance. "I've heard that line a million times. It's a solid talking point, but why would common criminals attack a U.S. Embassy outpost? Do you think they were trying to steal computers? Watches off the embassy staff? Cushions from the pool furniture?"

"They're criminals." Cordova's left eyebrow twitched. "I suppose they're going to steal whatever they can."

"Why choose a building guarded by U.S. Marines? And why do common criminals in Nigeria have RPGs?"

The congressman shot up in his chair. "Where did you get that information?"

"It wasn't from the watered-down report you sent me."

"Ms. Moreno, Lana—" he closed his eyes and took a deep breath "—I truly am sorry for the loss of your brother. He was a hero."

"He was a hero for getting murdered during a common robbery?"

"He was a hero for serving his country honorably, and I'm going to look into the possibility of naming a park…or something after him in our home town of Greenvale."

"A baseball field." Lana gazed at the pictures of Cordova's family that graced the wall behind him—his son in his baseball uniform and his daughter in a ballerina tutu. "Gil loved baseball and was a great player. He could've played some ball in college or the minor leagues, but he chose to enlist instead."

"Like I said, a true local hero."

Her eyes snapped back to Cordova's face. "He was a hero because he and his brothers in arms tried to protect that outpost from a planned attack. Whatever was going on there required more than three marines to guard it, and they deserved backup, a response from other military in the area. I know about that, too."

"I'm afraid the Committee is not going to open up an investigation based on some half-truths you learned from some anonymous source and your brother's journal that you haven't even read yet." Cordova's jawline hardened. "I've given you all the time I have today, Ms. Moreno, and you can run to the press all you like and paint me as the bad guy, but there's nothing more I can do for you."

She pushed out of the chair, her legs like lead beneath her, all the fight drained from her body. She automatically extended her hand across the desk. "Thank you for seeing me."

The congressman's face brightened as he squeezed her hand. "Anytime, Ms. Moreno, but make an appointment with Tessa next time and come alone."

"I will." When he released her hand, she avoided the temptation to wipe it on the seat of her jeans.

He circled around his desk and showed her out of his office door, a big smile on his face in case a camera or two lurked in the waiting room.

As she walked toward the exit, her knees weak and trembling, she nodded to Tessa behind her desk, clutching the edge, looking ready to bolt.

When Lana reached the door, Cordova called after her. "A baseball field, the Gil Moreno Field. I'll get right on it."

"Gilbert."

"Excuse me?"

"The Gilbert Moreno Baseball Field." She twisted the handle and bumped the door with her hip, pushing through the double doors.

The cold air slapped her face when she stepped onto the empty sidewalk and her nose started running. She shoved her hands in her pockets and turned the corner of Cordova's office, which occupied the end spot of a newer strip mall. He probably had nicer digs in DC.

Dragging her hand along the stucco wall of the building, she meandered toward the back alley. She couldn't do this anymore. She had nothing. She was going to fail her little brother when he needed her most.

She did a half turn and propped her shoulders against the wall, but her meeting with Cordova had sapped all her strength. Her knees giving out on her, she slid down the wall, the suede of her jacket scraping the stucco.

She ended in a crouch, dipping her head, the tears flowing freely down her face. "I'm sorry, Gil. You deserve so much more than a baseball field. You deserve the truth."

A footstep crunched beside her and she jerked up her head. A tall figure loomed over her, the sunlight creating a bright aura around the stranger's head.

Slowly he crouched before her, caught one of her tears as it dripped from her chin and said, "The truth just might get you killed, Lana."

Chapter Two

The raven-haired beauty in front of him dashed the back of her hand across her runny nose and smeared a streak of black mascara toward her ear, where a row of silver studs pierced the curve.

"Who the hell are you?" The tough words belied her trembling bottom lip, full with a juicy cherry tint.

Logan pulled back and blinked his eyes. He knew Lana Moreno was pretty, but he didn't expect her attractiveness, slightly muffled by a red nose and puffy eyes, to hit him like a sledgehammer.

He stuck out his hand. "I'm Logan Hess, your new best friend."

"I already have a best friend—" she narrowed her eyes "—and I already have a media contact. I'm working with Peyton Fletcher. She has my back."

"Oh, I doubt that." He dropped his hand onto his thigh, rubbing his knuckles across the denim of his jeans. "I'm not with any news organization."

The lips he'd been admiring flattened into a thin line. "Cordova's office? Is that why you were warning me about the truth? You did warn me, didn't you?"

"C'mon." He spread his arms. "Do I look like a politician?"

Her dark eyes tracked from the top of his head, flicked sideways across his leather jacket and traveled down his jeans. When she reached the silver tips of his black cowboy boots, her nostrils flared.

The inventory got him hot and bothered, and he willed Lana to keep her eyes pinned to his boots so she wouldn't notice his response to her assessment a little higher up.

He got his wish, as her eyes flew to his face. "As a matter of fact, you do kind of look like a politician—the smooth kind who tries to fit in with the locals with expensive designer duds no real Greenvale farmhand would ever wear…or could ever afford."

Ouch. His erection died as fast as it had come on.

Logan tipped back his head and laughed at the sky, laughed so hard he fell backward, his backside, covered by his nondesigner jeans, hitting the dirt. His hands went out behind him, and he wedged his palms against the ground to keep from falling back any farther.

"You're a pistol, little lady." He put on his best Texas drawl. "Would they say things like that, too?"

One side of her mouth twitched. "Yes, they would. That accent though, it sounds legit. Where'd you pick it up?"

"Same place I got these fancy duds." He slapped the side of his right boot. "Dallas. So, if you think you Greenvale, *California*, cowboys are the real deal, you're dreaming."

"Got me." Lana held up her hands. "But if you're not a reporter and you don't work for Cordova, I repeat my question. Who the hell are you? And don't say Logan Hess. That name means nothing to me."

He'd hoped she wouldn't recognize his name, but no report would ever reveal the names of a military unit.

"Let's try this again." Logan wiped his dusty palm against his shirt and held out his hand. "I'm Captain Logan Hess with U.S. Delta Force."

Her mouth formed an O but at least she took his hand this time in a firm grip, her skin rough against his. "I'm Lana Moreno, but you probably already know that, don't you?"

"I sure do." He jerked his thumb over his shoulder. "I saw your little impromptu news conference about an hour ago."

"But you knew who I was before that. You didn't track me down to compare cowboy boots." She jabbed him in the chest with her finger. "Did you know Gilbert?"

"Unfortunately, no." Lana didn't need to know just how unfortunate that really was. "Let's get out of the dirt and grab some lunch."

She tilted her head and a swathe of dark hair fell over her shoulder, covering one eye. The other eye scorched his face. "Why should I have lunch with you? What do you want from me? When I heard you were Delta Force, I thought you might have known Gilbert, might've known what happened at that outpost."

"I didn't, but I know *of* Gilbert and the rest of

them, even the assistant ambassador who was at the outpost. I can guarantee I know a lot more about the entire situation than you do from reading that redacted report they grudgingly shared with you."

"You *are* up-to-date. What are we waiting for?" Her feet scrambled beneath her as she slid up the wall. "If you have any information about the attack in Nigeria, I want to hear it."

"I thought you might." He rose from the ground, towering over her petite frame. He pulled a handkerchief from the inside pocket of his leather jacket and waved it at her. "Take this."

"Thank you." She blew her nose and mopped her face, running a corner of the cloth beneath each eye to clean up her makeup. "I suppose you don't want it back."

"You can wash it for me and return it the next time we meet."

That statement earned him a hard glance from those dark eyes, still sparkling with unshed tears, but he had every intention of seeing Lana Moreno again and again and however many times it took to pick her brain about why she believed there was more to the story than a bunch of Nigerian criminals deciding to attack an embassy outpost—a ridiculous cover story if he ever heard one.

About as ridiculous as the story of Major Rex Denver working with terrorists.

Her quest had to be motivated by more than grief over a brother. People didn't stage stunts like she just did in front of a congressman's office based on nothing.

"Sure, I'll wash it." Lana stuffed his handkerchief into the pocket of her suede jacket.

"My rental car's parked around the corner."

"That's nice." She shrugged her shoulders off the wall. "I'll take my truck over and meet you at the restaurant."

"Understood. You can't be too careful…especially you." Logan reached for his wallet. "Do you want to see my military ID before we go any further?"

She whipped around. "Why'd you say especially me? Come to think of it, why did you say the truth could get me killed?"

"I'll explain over lunch." He slipped his ID from his wallet and held it out to her, framed between his thumb at the bottom and two fingers at the top.

Her gaze bounced from the card to his face. "Your hair's shorter in the picture."

"Military cut." He ran a hand over the top of his head, the ends no longer creating a bristle.

"And lighter." She squinted at the photo on the card. "Almost blond."

Logan felt that warm awakening in his belly again under Lana's scrutiny. If this woman could turn him on just looking at his picture, he couldn't imagine what her touch would do to him. He shivered.

"This—" he tapped the card "—was taken in the summer. My hair tends to get darker in the winter. Any other questions? Do you want me to shed my jacket so you can check out my…weight?"

Lana's eyes widened for a second, and a pink blush

touched her mocha skin. "I'm not questioning you. The ID matches the man. Do you like Mexican?"

He blinked. He liked *this* Mexican. A lot.

"Food. Do you like Mexican food?" She stomped the dirt from her boots like a filly ready to trot.

"I'm from Texas. What do you think?"

"I've eaten Mexican food in Texas before, and if you think that salsa is hot…you're dreaming."

His lips twitched into a smile. If California salsa was as hot as Lana Moreno, he'd love it and ask for more. "Then I'm in for a treat because I like it hot and spicy."

Ignoring his innuendo, she turned her back on him and marched toward the street.

When they turned the corner and reached the front of the strip mall, someone in Congressman Cordova's office flicked the blinds at the window. Was the congressman afraid Lana would come storming back in?

She hadn't mentioned what she and Cordova discussed during their private conversation but judging from her tears after the meeting, it wasn't what she'd wanted.

She must've noticed the blinds, as well. Squaring her shoulders, she tossed her head, her dark mane shimmering down her back. "The restaurant's about ten minutes away."

She gave him the name and address and then hopped into an old white pickup truck with a flick of her fingers.

Could she reach the pedals of that monster? As

if to prove she could, she cranked on the engine and rattled past him.

Logan shook his head as he ducked into the small rental. He'd gotten more than he'd bargained for with Sergeant Gilbert Moreno's sister. He just hoped they could help each other, and for that, he needed to stay on Ms. Moreno's good side, which just might involve a little lying or at least some omission of the facts.

He plugged the restaurant's address into his phone and followed the directions that led him several miles away from the congressman's office. The buildings and streets on this side of town lacked the spiffy newness of the other area, but the restaurant stood out from the rest. It occupied a Spanish adobe building with a colorful sign out front and a small line at the door.

Logan parked his car and strode toward the entrance, his cowboy boots right at home with the *ranchera* music blaring from a bar two doors down from the restaurant.

Lana waved from the arched doorway of the restaurant, and he wove through the line of people waiting for a table.

"How long is the wait?"

"I already have a table in the back."

Logan raised his eyebrows. "Are you a regular here?"

"You could say that." She turned her head over her shoulder as she led him to their table, a small one that looked like an afterthought, tucked in next to the bar.

Logan reached past her to pull out a chair.

Putting a hand on the back of the chair, she said, "I'm going to wash my hands first."

"Probably not a bad idea." He turned his hands over and rubbed a thumb on his dirty palm.

"This way." She pointed down a short hallway behind the bar, and he followed her to the restrooms, his gaze slipping to her rounded derriere in her tight jeans.

Several minutes later, he made it back to the table, where two glasses of water waited for them, before she did.

Lana strolled from the kitchen, chatting with one of the waitresses, and Logan had a second chance to pull out her chair.

Lana thanked him as she took her seat. "Iced tea for me, Gabby."

"And for you?"

"Water is fine." Logan tapped the water glass on the table.

As soon as the waitress left, a busboy showed up with a basket of chips and a small bowl of salsa.

"Is the service always this good, or is it just you?"

"The service is always good here. It's one of the oldest Mexican restaurants in Greenvale, and one of the most popular—at least with the locals."

"And you're a local? Have you always lived in Greenvale?"

"My grandfather was a bracero in the Central Valley, worked the fields on a seasonal basis and then brought over my grandmother and their ten children. My father was third to the youngest."

"So, you have a big family here."

"Not here… Salinas. Most of them are still in Salinas. My father came to Greenvale to work with horses on a ranch. When the work became too much for him, he started cooking—here."

"Is he still in the kitchen?"

"He died two years ago."

"I'm sorry. Your mother?"

"My mother went back to her family in Mexico. My grandmother is ill and Mom takes care of her." She picked up a chip from the basket and broke it in two. "And you? Dallas native?"

"Born and raised outside of the Dallas–Fort Worth area." He dipped a chip in the salsa and crunched it between his teeth. He waved his hand in front of his mouth as he chewed it. "You weren't kidding. This stuff is hot."

"I can have Gabby bring a milder version for you, Tex."

He grabbed another chip and scooped up even more of the salsa. "Oh, them's fightin' words. Now it's a matter of pride."

Lana smiled, and their dark, little corner of the restaurant blazed with light.

"Competitive much?"

He nodded as he dabbed his runny nose with a napkin. Luckily Gabby saved him from stuffing his face with any more of the hot stuff as she approached their table and took their order.

When Gabby left, Logan took a sip of his water and hunched forward. "Tell me, Lana, why do you think there's more to the story than the government is telling us about the attack on the embassy?"

"Because my brother told me there was."

"He died in the attack."

She flinched. "He suspected something was going on before the attack."

"He communicated this to you?"

"We had a few face-to-face conversations on the computer after he got there. He didn't understand why they were at the outpost to begin with. There were a lot of secret comings and goings and a supply shed that they weren't allowed to enter."

"Who exactly was coming and going there?"

She lifted one shoulder. "Some Americans, some foreigners. The guards weren't briefed, and he didn't recognize any of them—except one."

"Who was that?" Logan's heart thumped so hard, Lana could probably hear it over the music playing in the background.

"A Major Rex Denver. The guards all knew him. They'd heard all about his exploits in Delta Force..." She snapped and aimed her index finger at him. "Delta Force, like you."

This was not one of the things Logan planned to lie to Lana about. "That's right. I know Major Denver. He was my squad leader before..."

"Before he turned traitor and went AWOL."

"That never happened." Logan slapped a palm on the table and a chip slid from the basket.

"You're trying to exonerate him. That's why you're interested in the attack on the embassy." She settled back in her chair and stirred her tea with the straw, the ice clinking against the glass. "Not sure the fact that Major Denver showed up at the outpost is going to do that. In fact, it makes him look guiltier if there was any hanky-panky going on at that compound."

"Not if he knew about the...hanky-panky and was there to investigate it himself."

Gabby brought their food. "Watch the plates. They're hot."

"Thanks, Gabby." Logan pointed his fork at the salsa dish. "Can you bring more salsa, please?"

"Of course." She swept the nearly depleted bowl from their table.

Lana smirked. "You don't have anything to prove, Logan."

"I know." He plunged his fork into his burrito and sliced off a corner. "It's growing on me."

She picked up one of her tacos and held it over her plate while the busboy delivered another bowl of salsa. "Maybe Denver's presence at the outpost triggered the attack, or maybe it was the questions he asked after his visit."

"How do you know he asked questions?"

"I know he asked Gil and the other marines a ton of questions while he was there. The guys were kind of in awe of him, but they couldn't give him any answers."

"Did Gil tell you what kinds of questions Denver was asking?"

"Mostly about that shed."

"I suppose you didn't record your sessions with your brother?"

"I didn't, but I'm sure he wrote down everything in his journal."

"He kept a journal?"

"Gil was always a good writer and I think he believed he had the makings of a book."

"Where's his journal, Lana?"

"On its way to me." She patted her chest. "The military is sending me his personal effects."

"You've already—" Logan swallowed "—buried him?"

Lana dropped her taco and crumpled her napkin in her hand. "Yes, they returned his body and we buried him with full military honors—a military that refuses to honor him now by telling the truth."

"I don't know if you can blame the military, Lana. There's something going on, something secretive, something so deep cover I don't think even the top brass knows what's happening."

"And you believe it has something to do with Major Denver."

"I know it does."

"Why did he take off? Why not stay and fight the charges against him?"

"Sometimes it's easier to wage a war on your own terms. Does that make sense?"

"Yes." She jabbed her straw into her glass so hard, a chip of ice flew onto the table and skittered toward him.

Logan dabbed at the ice with the tip of his finger.

"I think he could see the net closing in on him and he understood that it was a trap—especially for him. I'm sure wherever he is, he's fighting. He's doing it his own way."

"I can understand that."

She gazed over his shoulder as if at something in the distance, and he wondered what battles Lana had undertaken on her own.

Several minutes later, Gabby slipped the check out of her pocket and waved it over the table. "Anything else?"

"Not for me. Logan?"

"Anything more than that burrito?" He plucked the check from Gabby's fingers. "No way."

She picked up their plates and spun away, calling over her shoulder. "See you next time, Lana."

Lana stretched out her arm to him and wiggled her fingers. "How much do I owe?"

"I'll take care of it on one condition."

"What's that?"

"You keep me updated on Gil's journal and anything else you find."

"And you do the same."

"Deal."

"It seems like we'll be helping each other, so we can split the check, too."

"I'm the one who suggested lunch. You can get the next one."

She plunged her hand into her purse and pulled out a wallet. "Let me get the tip."

"Don't worry. I'll be generous with the tip." He

added a few more bills to the pile and held it out to her. "Is this okay?"

"More than generous."

"You're kind of a control freak, aren't you?"

"You could say that." She stood up and pulled her jacket from the back of her chair. "Where are you staying?"

"The Greenvale Inn and Suites back by the congressman's office, but I'm not going there right now." He reached the front door of the restaurant before she did and held it open for her.

"Where are you going?"

"I'm following you back to your place. You said you were expecting a delivery of your brother's possessions any day, and I'm going to hold you to your word."

"All right." She flicked up the collar of her jacket. "I want to show you something in that report, anyway. Have you read it?"

"I've seen bits and pieces of it, not the entire report."

"The report *is* bits and pieces. There's so much redaction, it's hard to read."

He could believe that. There would be secrecy surrounding an embassy outpost like that even without an attack. "Your address?"

"Just follow me. It'll be easier."

He did follow her, right to her truck, and opened the heavy door after she'd unlocked it.

She placed one boot on the running board and

hopped into the driver's seat. "It's about a forty-minute drive."

"I'll be right behind you."

He followed her out of town and along the two-lane highway. He hadn't given too much thought to Lana's housing situation, but didn't expect her to live out in the boonies like this.

Farmland rolled past his window, and occasionally he got a whiff of fresh manure, a smell that reminded him of home.

After about forty minutes of driving, the right indicator on Lana's truck flashed on and off and she slowed down. She turned and drove the truck between two posts onto a small paved road.

As Logan took his car through the posts, he tried to read the writing carved on the sides but it was too small. Lana lived on a ranch. Was it hers? Her husband's?

The thought of a husband lurking beyond the gate up ahead socked him in the gut, but he brushed it aside. If Lana Moreno had a husband, she wouldn't be running around on her own trying to get closure on Gil. And if she had a husband and he allowed her to do this on her own, the guy didn't deserve her.

As Lana's truck approached the main gate to the ranch, Logan threw his car into Park and jumped out. He jogged to the gate, unhitched it and swung it wide.

Lana waved as she drove through and then waited for him while he followed with his car. He pulled up behind her, left his car idling, closed the gate and slid back into his rental.

He kept after her as she wound up the road past a horse riding ring and a pasture. Her truck rattled past the big house that had a later-model truck than hers and a minivan parked in the front.

He didn't take her for a minivan type, anyway. She kept driving toward a stand of trees and then curved around them, pulling alongside a much-smaller house than the one in front and hidden from the view of the road.

He left his rental car several feet behind her truck. When he got out, she was halfway to the porch.

"I think it's here." Her boots clattered on the wooden steps of the front porch.

By the time he joined her, she'd sunk beside a box by the front door and had slid a knife along the taped seam.

As she made a grab for one loose flap, he said, "Let me get it inside for you first."

She scrambled to her feet, as he wrapped his arms around the box and hoisted it against his chest. With hands that could barely hold on to her key chain, she fumbled at the lock before he heard a click and the door swung open.

She stood to the side. "Put it in the middle of the floor."

His boots clumped against the hardwood floor as he made his way to a throw rug in the middle of the room. Crouching, he allowed the box to slip from his grasp until it settled on the floor.

Lana fell to her knees beside it, knife clutched in her hand. She ran it along the other seam and peeled back the lid. She stopped, gripping either side of the box, her eyes closed.

"Are you all right?" Logan touched her hand. "Do you want to do this on your own? I can step outside."

Her eyelids flew open and one tear glistened on the edge of her long lashes. "It's okay. It's the smell, you know? It came at me all at once—his smell."

Logan inhaled deeply. Lana smelled her brother, but another scent hit him and resonated deep in his core. "It's the smell of war."

Hunching over the box, she buried both of her hands inside and pulled out some clothing. She placed a stack of clothes on the floor, smoothing her hands over the shirt folded on top. She dived in again and again, withdrawing toiletries, books and personal items.

As the pile of Gil's things grew around her, her movements grew more and more frantic until she withdrew the final item from the box—Gil's beret.

She collapsed against the base of the couch, clutching the hat to her chest, her eyes dark slits. "They stole it. Somebody took Gil's journal."

Chapter Three

Lana kicked the empty box with her foot, flipping it over. She should've known someone would snatch Gil's journal. Maybe if she hadn't blabbed to anyone who would listen about what she knew and how, Gil's journal wouldn't have come under any scrutiny. She'd led them right to it—and the only proof she had that the attack on the outpost wasn't random.

"You're sure it's not in one of these smaller pouches?" Logan poked at Gil's stuff with his finger, toppling one of the piles.

"I looked in each one as I pulled it out, but you're welcome to do it again." She folded her arms over Gil's beret and dipped her head, the scratchy wool tickling her chin. "I messed up. I shouldn't have mentioned that journal to anyone."

"Maybe there's another box on its way. Maybe the mail person delivered the second box to the house in the front. Does that ever happen?" Logan righted the empty box and placed his hands inside, as if he thought there might be a false bottom.

"The mail person doesn't make mistakes but

my stuff does have a habit of winding up at the big house." Lana clenched her teeth at the thought of Bruce pawing through Gil's belongings.

Logan sprang to his feet and extended his hand to her. "Do you want to ask them?"

"You're coming with me?"

He cocked his head. "If you want me to."

She couldn't wait to parade Captain Logan Hess in front of Bruce, even though she couldn't pass off Logan as anything more than a friend, not even that, really, but she'd relish the expression on Bruce's face when he got a look at Logan and his rippling muscles. Not that she could see those muscles under his shirt—but she could imagine them and she had a wild imagination.

"Of course I want you to. You don't want to stay here by yourself, do you?" She grabbed his hand, and he pulled her to her feet.

She dropped the beret on the couch, but didn't drop Logan's hand—not yet. The strength and warmth of his fingers sent a zap of courage through her body, and she sorely needed some of that right now.

This must be how it feels to have someone on your side.

He squeezed her hand. "Are you okay? That had to be rough going through your brother's personal effects."

"I'm all right. I'll feel better once I get my hands on his journal."

Logan had taken off his jacket when they'd walked into the house and he grabbed it from the back of the chair. She hadn't bothered shedding hers but zipped it up now to meet the cold—and Bruce McGowan.

As they tromped down her driveway toward the main house, Logan said, "I'm assuming the people in the big house own this ranch."

"They do."

"And you do...what?"

"I train horses here. My father worked for the current owner's father, Douglas McGowan, who kept me on after my father went to the restaurant. Douglas died just a few months after my father's death."

"So, you've been here two years on your own. You're lucky. You must like it to have stayed on."

A muscle twitched in her jaw, and she rubbed it away. "It's a job and I need a job. I'm sending money to my mom in Mexico, so she can take care of *abuelita*."

"You're saying you don't like it?"

"I like the horses." She put a finger to her lips as they rounded the corner of the yellow house.

She climbed the two steps to the porch, and the familiar butterflies swirled around her stomach as she jabbed her knuckle against the doorbell.

The bell rang deep in the house, and Lana squared her shoulders and shoved her hands in her pockets, knowing Bruce was peering at her through the peephole, or soon would be.

Seconds later, the door swung open and Bruce's big frame filled the doorway. His face broke into a grin. "Lana-Madonna, what brings you to my castle? You must..."

His words trailed off as the step behind Lana squeaked and Logan hovered behind her.

"Bruce, this is Logan Hess. Logan, Bruce Mc-Gowan."

As Bruce lurched past her to grab Logan's hand, his shoulder brushed hers.

"Nice to meet you, Logan. Friend of our little horse trainer?"

Lana held her breath as Logan seemed to suck in his with a sharp breath.

"Yeah." Logan dropped his hand from Bruce's and placed it on the small of her back.

Bruce's gaze flicked to the gesture, and then the smile, a bit stiffer this time, returned to his face. "What can I do you for on this fine winter afternoon?"

"I received a delivery today—a box—and I was wondering if by any *chance* there was a second box delivered here by mistake."

"Those mail people—give them one job to do and you'd think they could do it right instead of screwing it up all the time." Bruce glanced at Logan and shrugged. "They're always delivering Lana's mail up here to the big house."

"Yeah, funny how that works though. I never seem to get *your* mail. Anyway, did you get a box delivered?"

"Nope."

"Did you pick up the mail or did Dale? Where is Dale?"

"She's upstairs…resting." Bruce's jawline hardened. "Dale didn't pick up the mail. She's pretty much been…resting since she took the kids to school—and they're still there in case you're wondering."

"I figured that." The butterflies returned and she pressed a hand against her belly. "You'll let me know if you get something of mine."

"Always, Lana. Anytime you need anything from me, well *almost* anything, my door's always open." Bruce winked.

Logan's body, just behind hers, tensed, his fingers curling into her hip.

Bruce stepped back inside the house as his face momentarily lost its ruddy color. "Nice to meet you, Logan. Any friend of Lana's is a friend of ours. You have a good day now."

He practically slammed the door in their faces, and Lana released a pent-up breath.

She pivoted on the porch and marched to her house with Logan hot on her heels, but silent.

When they reached her porch, he grabbed her arm. "What the hell was that all about? Who does that guy think he is? He's lucky he still has his front teeth after the way he talked to you. Our *little* horse trainer? I'm surprised you didn't smack him after that one."

"He's my employer." She lifted a shoulder. "And my landlord. He and Dale let me live here for free. It was an arrangement his father had with mine, but I'm sure Bruce could end that arrangement anytime he wanted, especially since he's selling off most of his horses."

"He clearly doesn't want to end the arrangement. He likes having you at his beck and call, doesn't he?"

"You caught that, huh?" She dragged her lower lip between her teeth. She would hate for Logan to believe she and Bruce had anything between them—like the ranching community here believed.

"It's just as clear to me that you don't want to be here. So why not move? Find another job?"

She swallowed the lump in her throat. "It's not that easy to find a job as a horse trainer, Logan, and free rent? Impossible. I have an advantageous setup here and putting up with Bruce once in a while is worth it."

And worth it for the other big perk.

Logan narrowed his eyes. "What does putting up with Bruce once in a while entail? Does he steal your mail?"

"That's one of the little games he plays with me." Lana sank to the top step and curled an arm around the wooden banister post. "He takes pieces of my mail, claiming it was a mistake on the part of the mail person, and then lets me know he has them to force me to go up to the big house."

"Tell him to put the mail back in your mailbox." Logan took a seat beside her on the porch, his shoulder bumping hers, which caused a completely different feeling to surge through her body from the one occasioned by Bruce doing the same thing.

"He always has an excuse why he can't do that. Bottom line—if I want my mail, I have to get it from him."

"He sounds like an ass. He *is* an ass and needs his kicked."

Lana's lips curved into a smile. "I'd like to see that, but for now I just avoid him as much as possible."

"Do you believe he doesn't have a second box of Gil's?"

"I'm not sure if I do or not. Your presence threw him for a loop. It wouldn't be any fun for him to invite me in and give me the box if you were by my side. That's something he'd prefer to do without an audience."

Logan's eyebrows collided over his nose. "Has he ever gotten physical with you? Do you have anything to fear from him other than his slimy words and manner?"

Lana ran her tongue around the inside of her mouth, the sour taste almost gagging her. "Only one time."

"What did he do?" Logan's body vibrated beside hers as if he were ready to take on Bruce right here and now.

"He…he put his hands around my waist and pulled me in for a kiss." She rolled her lips inward at the memory and put her hand over her mouth.

"Bastard. Did you slug him?"

"I was too shocked to react quickly enough. I did push him away and told him I'd report him to Dale if he ever tried that again."

"What did he do?"

"Laughed, but he never tried it again."

"Yet." Logan kicked at a rock with the toe of his

boot. "What's the story with his wife and why is she resting?"

"Dale's an alcoholic. They have...two adorable kids, but Dale spends most of her time hitting the bottle and partying with her friends." She pinned her hands between her knees and tapped her boots together. "Honestly, I don't think she cares what Bruce does. I'm pretty sure she has an affair or two under her belt."

"So to speak." Logan smirked. "Doesn't sound like you have much leverage with the wife."

"Yeah, except Bruce doesn't want to give Dale any excuse for a divorce. They don't have a prenup. and Bruce stands to lose a lot—half of everything— in a divorce. That's why he puts up with her behavior, too."

"Sounds like a great marriage, a match made in hell, but I don't give a damn about Bruce or Dale or their hellish marriage. I *do* give a damn about your safety and the way he treats you."

She patted Logan's thigh. "Thanks. He's not going to try anything else. He just plays his little games with me and enjoys watching me squirm because he knows I have nowhere else to go."

"I got a totally different vibe from you when I watched you outside of Congressman Cordova's office. I didn't see you as someone who'd take guff from anyone." He turned on the step and took her by the shoulders. "You need to get out of here, Lana. Find another job, move. This is unhealthy."

She flattened a hand against her stomach. She

hated for anyone to see her as weak, especially a man like Logan Hess, who probably charged through life on his own terms. But she'd been weak plenty of times in her life, and she didn't want Logan to know about those times, either.

Resting her head against the post, she asked, "Are you married, Logan? Do you have…children?"

His head jerked. "No."

She ignored the little sigh of relief that sprang to her lips and continued, "Have you ever had anyone dependent on you?"

"My Delta Force team. We're dependent on each other."

"If you had to do something you didn't like, had to just suck it up and get on with it to protect one of your team members, you'd do it, wouldn't you?"

"I'd do anything for them." His thumbs pressed against her collarbone through her jacket. "What are you getting at?"

"That's me." She waved an arm toward the ranch. "Here."

His gaze shifted over her shoulder to take in the expanse of the ranch. "You're protecting someone here?"

"I have responsibilities here. I'm sending money to my mom and my grandmother in Mexico. I can't just quit work. I have horses here…relationships." She tossed her head like one of those horses, flicking her hair over her shoulder. "I can handle Bruce Mc-Gowan. It's the U.S. Government I'm worried about."

"Okay. I'm sorry." He dropped his hands from her

shoulders. "It's none of my business how you conduct yours. I hate guys like McGowan, who abuse their power."

Logan's green eyes burned with a passion that had to go deeper than what he'd just witnessed between her and Bruce. Any injustice seemed to instill in Logan a desire to correct it. That same feeling must be driving him to exonerate Major Denver.

"I appreciate your concern. Like I said, I can handle Bruce...*and* Smith & Wesson if it comes to that."

The crease between his eyebrows vanished. "That's good to hear not only because of Bruce's attentions, but because you are kind of isolated out here."

"There are some quarters for the ranch hands behind the stables. It's not as isolated as you might think."

"Do you mind if I take another look at that box?"

She pushed up from the porch and dusted off the seat of her jeans. "C'mon back in."

Once inside the house, Logan crouched beside the box she'd sliced open with such anticipation. He studied the tape hanging from the flaps, and then shoved the box toward her. "Does that look retaped to you?"

Lana ran her fingertip along the tape and looked up. "It could've been. Do you think someone opened the box, searched it and taped it back up?"

"Could've happened. Someone did a slick job of it if that's what occurred, but there's some roughness that could be some cardboard ripped off the box."

"It's worse than if McGowan is holding on to a second box, isn't it? The motivation is a hundred times more sinister." She pinged the side of the box with her fingernail. "And if someone took Gil's journal, I'll never have any proof that his death was part of some organized attack."

"Lana, are you sure your brother kept a journal?"

"I'm positive. He always did, and since he suspected something amiss on this assignment, he wouldn't have quit at this precise moment."

"Unless he sensed the danger of keeping a journal."

"What if I never find it? What if it's gone forever?" She fell to her knees next to the piles of Gil's belongings and ran her hands over the items. "I won't be able to help you with your investigation, either."

"Don't worry about that." Logan rose to his feet. "I just wanted to touch base with you to find out why you were so adamant in the belief that there was something more to that attack. I didn't expect you to have any proof...just a sister's grief."

A hot tear coursed down her cheek and she let it drop off her chin. That's twice she'd allowed this man to see her cry—some kind of record.

In two steps, he was towering above her and gently urged her to her feet. She swayed as she rose beside him, and he enfolded her in his arms.

"I'm so sorry for your loss." He whispered the words in her ear.

She nodded against his solid chest. "Thank you. I know as a serviceman, you understand maybe more than most do."

Sniffling, she pulled away from his warm comfort,

trying to avoid wiping her nose on his shirt. Trying not to be too dependent.

He stepped back, leaving a cold void between them. "I—I'd better get going. I'll leave you my cell phone number in case anything else comes up, and you do the same."

"How long will you be staying in Greenvale?" Now, suddenly having that journal in her hands meant more than uncovering the mysterious circumstances behind the marine guards' deaths. It meant keeping in contact with Logan Hess. Once she had nothing to offer him, he'd take off in search of the next clue.

How quickly that feeling had come back—that she had to have something to offer to make someone stick around. She hadn't learned anything.

"I'll be here for a few days. I hope to talk to Congressman Cordova myself."

She brushed a hand across her wet cheek. "Maybe I can reciprocate and buy you lunch while you're still here."

"I'd like that." He jerked his thumb in the direction of the big house. "You'll be okay here?"

"I live here. I'll be fine."

Five minutes later, she pressed the piece of paper with Logan's cell phone number on it to her heart and watched him fold his large frame into the little rental car that looked too small for him.

She lifted her hand as he went around the line of trees and disappeared from view. Then she spun around and dived into Gil's possessions, returning most of his things to the box.

After packing away Gil's belongings, checking on the few horses left at the ranch and eating dinner, Lana made some tea and curled up with her laptop.

Her activity had driven Logan from her thoughts—temporarily. She'd better get Logan out of her head—at least until their lunch. He'd be on his way soon, and she'd be among his vague memories and one of many people he'd encountered while trying to clear his commander's name.

But a girl could dream—or at least do a little investigating on her own.

She powered on her laptop and entered Logan's name and Dallas, Texas, in a search engine, her eyes widening at the number of articles scrolling down her display. No wonder Logan believed she could just pick up and leave. No wonder he felt a person shouldn't have to put up with an uncomfortable situation.

Easy for him to lecture her about principles—he had all the money in the world to buy them.

Sighing, she snapped shut the lid of her computer and swept it off her lap. Now she had to try all over again to get Logan off her brain, and after discovering more about him that became even more important. Given Logan's background and situation, he could never be right for her.

She got another cup of tea and settled back on the couch, this time losing herself in the English accents and costumes of a period drama on TV. As she clicked onto the next episode, frantic banging on her front door disturbed the English countryside.

Knots tightened in her belly. She hoped none of

the horses had been taken ill. She kicked off the blanket wrapped around her waist and strode toward the front door.

With her hand on the doorknob, she peeked through the window and her heart skipped several beats as she looked at the tear-streaked faces of Carla and Daniel McGowan. Bruce had better not be on one of his rampages, terrifying the children.

Lana jerked open the door. "What's wrong, kids? Where are your parents?"

Carla placed a hand on her little brother's shoulder just like Lana used to do with Gil. "Daddy's not home. They've taken Mama. We hid in the closet."

Lana's fluttering heart banged against her chest. She gathered the children toward her and into the house and slammed the door. "What are you talking about? Who took your mother?"

She crouched in front of Daniel and wrapped her arms around his shaking body. Had Dale gotten involved in drugs along with her drinking? Bruce's wife had been associating with some rough characters in the dive bars she favored.

"I don't know, Lana." Carla sniffled and wiped the back of her hand across her nose. "Mama was downstairs watching TV. I heard the doorbell ring and then loud noises when she went to answer the door. When I looked through the banister from upstairs, two men were in the house and they were hurting Mama."

Lana put a hand to her throat. Dear God, what had Carla witnessed? "Is that when you hid?"

Carla nodded. "I made Daniel get away from the stairs and we hid in the closet."

"Did these men look for you?" Keeping Daniel by her side, Lana walked backward toward the kitchen and her phone charging on the counter. Carla followed them.

"They stayed downstairs, yelling at Mama. I kept quiet." She patted her brother's head. "And I kept Daniel quiet, too. Then I heard the front door close and I couldn't hear anything else. When we went downstairs, they were gone—Mama, too."

Lana held up her phone and her hand had only a slight tremble. "Have you called 911 yet? Your father?"

"I couldn't find Mama's cell phone and I didn't want to stay in the house, so we ran over here." Carla dropped her lashes. "Is that okay?"

"Okay? That's super amazing. That's precisely what you should've done." Lana blinked back her tears.

Lana called 911 and told them as much of the story as she could. Bruce might've preferred to handle this on his own without the police, especially if one of Dale's lovers or some drug dealer had her, but he'd just have to suck up the embarrassment on this one. It sounded like Dale was in serious trouble.

"The police are on their way, sweetie." Lana curled her free arm around Carla's stiff little body, inhaling the sweet scent from her hair. "You are so brave, Carla. Did you hear what the men were saying to your mama? The police are going to ask you some questions."

"They kept asking her about a gerbil. Where was the gerbil? Where had she put the gerbil? We don't have a gerbil."

"Of course not." Lana bit her lower lip. That made no sense. "Did you get a look at the men?"

"They had masks on." Carla formed her fingers into circles and put them over her eyes. "Like when you go skiing and it's really cold."

Daniel had been patting Lana on the back, so Lana squeezed him tighter. "Are you okay, Daniel? You're very brave, too."

She didn't want to play favorites.

"They didn't say *gerbil*, Carla."

"What, sweetie?" Taking Daniel's hand, Lana sat back on her heels. "You didn't hear *gerbil*?"

"They didn't say, where's the gerbil? They said, where's the journal? They hit Mama on the face and said, 'Give us the journal, bitch.'"

Chapter Four

As the sirens wailed their approach, Lana shoved open the gate and pulled her jacket tighter, the gun heavy in her pocket. She'd left Carla and Daniel with a few of the ranch hands at her house. The kids had been afraid to go back to their own house, and she'd been afraid to leave them alone at hers.

And after Daniel's insistence that the word *gerbil* Carla heard was actually *journal*, she'd just been afraid.

She'd tried calling Bruce a few more times, but he'd gone radio silent—probably on one of his own benders, which involved gambling as opposed to drinking—not the best environment for the children.

When the squad cars' lights illuminated the road to the ranch, Lana stood in front of the gate and waved her arms over her head.

She ran to the driver's-side door of the first car to roll through the gate. "The house is up ahead. I'll meet you there."

"I'm Officer Jacobs. You're Lana Moreno, right? Why don't you hop in and tell me what's going on?"

Lana scurried in front of the police car, squinting against the lights and keeping her jacket close to her body so the officer wouldn't see her gun. She slid into the passenger seat.

"There's been a kidnapping, Dale McGowan, the owner of the ranch."

"I know the McGowans. Was Mr. McGowan present?"

"Bruce is out. I haven't been able to reach him yet."

Jacobs nodded, his jaw tight.

He probably knew Bruce from a few domestic violence calls they'd received—from Bruce. Dale had been known to throw a vase or two in a drunken rage, and while Bruce didn't want to air their dirty laundry in public, he also didn't want to be caught with his pants down if Dale ever did sue him for divorce. He'd wanted to have some ammunition ready in case that day ever came.

Maybe now it never would.

Hunching her shoulders, Lana hugged herself. All because someone was looking for Gil's journal.

"The kids okay?"

"They're fine. They hid, although the…kidnappers never made any effort to search the rest of the house for any other family members."

"Maybe they knew Mr. McGowan was out, and they didn't want to harm the children."

"Maybe." Lana slid a sideways glance at the officer. He'd already landed on his first suspect—the husband. She wouldn't put it past Bruce to get rid of Dale to avoid the alimony, but not over a missing journal.

As they reached the house, the other squad car pulled up beside them and another car roared in behind them. Jacobs exited his vehicle, his hand hovering over his service revolver on his hip as he turned to face the headlights of the oncoming car.

Lana blew out a breath when the little rental squealed to a stop. "It's okay. He's a friend of mine."

Logan bolted from the car and swooped toward her. "Are you all right?"

"I'm fine. Dale McGowan's been kidnapped." She leaned toward Logan. "How'd you know about this?"

"I was in the lobby bar of my hotel and word spread like wildfire that there was trouble at the McGowan ranch." He took both of her hands. "I'm sorry for Mrs. McGowan, but I'm glad it's not you."

"Don't get ahead of yourself."

Logan squeezed her hands. "What does that mean?"

"Stop! Don't come any closer." The officer's voice cut through their conversation.

Lana spun around to see the ranch hands, Humberto and Leggy, frozen in the white spotlight from the squad car, the kids clamped in front of them.

She disentangled her hands from Logan's. "These two men are with the ranch. I left them with the McGowan children at my house."

Both officers approached the ranch hands and when they'd determined the men knew nothing beyond what she'd told them, they dismissed them.

Jacobs cupped his hand and gestured toward her. "Lana, take the kids into the house and sit with them while we question them. Someone was able to reach their father, and he's on his way."

Taking a step back, she grabbed Logan's sleeve. "I need my friend with me, too."

As she and Logan followed the officers and the kids to the McGowan house, Logan dipped his head to hers and whispered in her ear, "What's going on? Do you have something more to tell me?"

"Daniel, the boy, said the kidnappers were asking his mother about a journal."

Logan cursed softly. "Do the police know any of this yet?"

"Not yet, but I'm gonna give 'em an earful."

The officers gently led Carla and Daniel through an account of what they heard and saw.

Lana gave the kids encouraging smiles as her attention bounced between them and Logan as he wandered around the living room. He sauntered to the grand piano and picked up a framed photograph of Dale McGowan.

He slowly turned toward her, clutching the picture in his hands. He pointed at her and then pointed to the picture of Dale, who could've been her sister.

Lana nodded. Her resemblance to Dale had come in handy more than once.

When Daniel got to his part of the story, correcting Carla about the word the kidnappers were repeating, Lana cleared her throat.

Officer Jacobs glanced up. "Do you have something to add, Lana?"

"I—I think I know what might have happened."

She twisted her fingers in front of her. How crazy was this going to sound? "I'm expecting a journal from my brother. H-he died overseas recently. If you know Dale McGowan, you know we look alike. I'm thinking this is a case of mistaken identity and Dale's kidnappers were really after me…and my brother's journal."

Jacobs blinked. "Why would anyone want your brother's journal to the point of kidnapping and violence?"

"I think it contains some classified information, or information certain people don't want released."

Officer Zander, the female officer, pointed at Lana. "I saw you on the news tonight outside of Congressman Cordova's office. You think this kidnapping is related to what you were talking about on TV?"

Jacobs put a hand to his head as if she'd just ruined his case. "Lana…"

The front door burst open and Bruce charged across the threshold. "Kids? Kids, are you okay?"

Carla and Daniel broke away from the officers and ran at their father, who gathered both of them in his arms. Tears stung Lana's nose and she rubbed the tip.

Bruce pinned Jacobs with a hard stare over the top of Carla's head. "They're not hurt, are they? My wife's scumbag associates didn't hurt *my* children, did they?"

"*Your* kids are fine, Bruce, shaken up." Lana stood up, hands on her hips. "Where were you?"

"Who are you, the detective on the case?" Bruce

glared at her and shifted his gaze to Logan, his glare turning even icier.

Jacobs stood up, nervously tapping his pencil against a notebook. "The kids ran to Lana's house, Mr. McGowan. She called 911 and made sure they were safe. Are you saying your wife had…associates who would kidnap her?"

"It could all be a ruse." Bruce sliced one hand through the air. "Maybe Dale thought this would be a good way to spend a few days away from her home and children."

"Are you done with the kids, Officer Jacobs? Maybe they should go to bed." Lana shot Bruce a hard look and ran her finger across her throat.

Carla and Daniel didn't need to hear their father attacking their mother's character, although they'd probably heard it all before.

Officer Zander asked, "Kids, do you have anything else you want to add?"

They shook their heads and clung to their father. Of course they'd cling to their father. He provided them with everything they desired—except maybe a happy, peaceful home.

Bruce hoisted up Daniel with one arm and put his other hand on Carla's head. "I'll tuck them in, and then I can give you the lowdown."

When Bruce had disappeared up the long curving staircase, Lana turned back to Jacobs. "I don't know what Bruce thinks this is all about, but I'm telling you if the kidnappers were asking Dale about a journal, they thought she was me."

Jacobs exchanged a look with Zander and blew out a breath. "If they were after you and this journal, why didn't they go to your house instead of this one? Yours is just back behind the trees, isn't it?"

"You can't see my house from the drive, even if you know it's there. They probably just know I live at the McG Ranch, saw the house, saw Dale, who looks an awful lot like me, and started questioning her."

"Why the kidnapping?" Officer Zander got up and joined Logan by the piano. She plucked up the framed photo of Dale and studied it. "There *is* a strong resemblance."

Logan, who'd been trying to blend in with the furniture, cleared his throat. "If Dale was insisting she didn't have the journal and didn't know what they were talking about, they'd want to interrogate her further, pressure her—without interruption. They didn't want to be surprised by a husband or children or anyone else on the ranch."

Lana shoved her hand in her pocket, tracing the butt of the gun with her fingertip. *Pressure? Interrogate?* She didn't like the sound of those words at all. Poor Dale. Lana felt a stab of guilt for involving Dale in her life yet again.

Jacobs shook his head. "I don't know, Lana. That sounds crazy, but we won't discount it as a motive. We'll need to talk to Bruce more. It sounds like Dale is in over her head with some shady individuals."

"And Lana isn't?" Logan drove his finger into the top of the piano. "If the boy, Daniel, is right, the men who abducted his mother were demanding answers about a journal. Lana knows about a journal. Dale doesn't."

"That's if Daniel heard them correctly. The kid was scared."

Logan rolled his eyes. "So, he just happened to hear the word *journal*?"

Officer Jacobs turned his head toward Lana. "Did you maybe ask the kids if the men said anything about a journal?"

"No."

"I don't know what stories Lana's been telling, Jacobs, but I'll tell you all about my wife." Bruce lumbered down the stairs brushing his hands together.

"Are the children okay?" Officer Zander walked away from the piano, taking the framed picture of Dale with her.

"The kids are fine. Daniel's already asleep and Carla's in bed. It might take her longer to fall asleep after what she witnessed."

Lana took a step forward. "Should I…?"

"No." Bruce sliced a hand through the air. "She'll be fine. I'll check on her after I talk to the police."

Zander held up the photo of Dale. "Do you want us to use this picture of your wife?"

"That'll work…if she wants to be found." Bruce stationed himself in front of the wet bar and lifted the lid from a crystal decanter. "Drink, anyone?"

"C'mon, Bruce." Jacobs jerked his finger between his chest and Zander's. "You know we're on duty."

"Then I guess it's just me because I don't think Lana and her…friend need to be here anymore, do they?"

"Unless you can tell me anything more about who might want this journal of yours, Lana, I think we're done."

Logan crossed his arms and widened his stance in the middle of the room. "Isn't it enough that she's in danger from these people? If they brazenly snatched Mrs. McGowan out of her own home with her children upstairs, don't you think they'd do the same to Lana once they realize their mistake?"

Jacobs twitched at Bruce's snort from across the room and said, "We don't know for sure what happened here tonight. I'm going to call in the crime scene investigators to look at any prints in the house or tire tracks out front."

"Except our prints are all over the crime scene now, aren't they?" Logan held his hands in front of him, spreading his fingers. "And our tire tracks."

Bruce lifted his drink and swirled the amber liquid in the glass. "You two can leave now while I tell the officers the *real* reason for this so-called kidnapping."

Lana stood up and put her hand on Logan's forearm, corded with tension. "Let's go. Hopefully they won't hurt Dale once they realize she's not me. I'm glad the kids are okay."

When they got outside, Lana puffed out a breath, watching it take shape in the frosty air. "It was scary enough when Carla and Daniel showed up on my doorstep and told me their mother had been forcibly removed from their home in a kidnapping, but when Daniel said they'd been badgering her about a journal, I knew. I knew they'd come for me."

She grabbed the front of Logan's shirt. "I'm not crazy, am I? You thought the same thing."

"Of course, especially once I saw a photo of Dale McGowan. The two men who snatched Dale must've had a picture of you or had seen you on the news and had the address of the McG Ranch in Greenvale and went from there. They probably didn't pay any attention to Dale's disclaimers about the journal because why would you admit to having it?"

Lana's boots crunched the gravel as she made her way back to her house, tucked safely behind the trees. And Logan's boots crunched right beside hers. "Will they hurt Dale once they discover their mistake? *Will* they discover their mistake?"

"If Dale can't convince them they have the wrong woman, the news will. I'm sure the kidnapping of Bruce McGowan's wife is going to be splashed all over town tomorrow."

"I-if they keep their ski masks on and Dale can't identify them, there's no reason for them to kill her or even harm her, right?"

Logan rubbed a circle on her back and it shouldn't have given her so much comfort, but he had that effect on her.

"I know you're worried about Dale and I am, too, but I'm more concerned about you. They must really want Gil's journal to go to these extremes to get their hands on it." He paused on the porch step below her, which still wasn't enough to put them eye-to-eye. "Who did you tell about the journal?

Have you mentioned it in any of your interviews or news conferences?"

"I might have mentioned it once or twice." She dropped her head and kicked the side of the porch with the toe of her boot. "Pretty stupid, huh?"

He wedged a finger beneath her chin, tilting up her head. "If I didn't realize the lengths someone was willing to travel to get that journal, how could you possibly know? Don't beat yourself up about it. Your safety is of greater concern right now."

"I have that covered." Lana patted her pocket.

Logan grabbed the outside of her jacket pocket, juggling the heft of her gun with his palm. "When did you arm yourself?"

"Before I went to the big house."

"Good idea." Taking a step down, he tilted back his head. "Do you have any security here? Cameras? Light sensors?"

"No. Bruce doesn't even have cameras at the big house. I don't know why, since he's always worried about the ranch hands stealing from him." She pressed her lips together.

"That's no way to run a ranch. Does he have reason to worry?"

"Absolutely not. You saw Humberto and Leggy. They'd do anything for Bruce's family, anything for this ranch."

"He's generally a miserable person who makes everyone else miserable. Like I said, no way to run a ranch."

"That's Bruce."

A pair of footsteps crunched in the darkness and Lana shoved her hand back in her pocket as Logan turned and blocked her body with his.

"Lana, you okay?"

Her shoulders slumped and she put a hand on Logan's arm. "It's Humberto. I'm fine, Humberto."

The ranch hand stepped forward, Leggy behind him. "Do the police know who took Mrs. McGowan?"

"Not yet. Bruce is with the police now, giving them all kinds of reasons why his wife might've been kidnapped—all her fault, I'm sure."

Leggy pointed at Logan. "Is this guy staying with you tonight, Lana?"

She sucked in a quick breath. *She wished.* "This is Logan Hess. Logan, this is Humberto Garcia and Larry Kroger, otherwise known as Leggy."

Logan jumped from the porch and shook the men's hands. "I wasn't invited to spend the night, but I'd be okay with you two standing guard."

"Don't be ridiculous. They're not going to come back tonight after we called the police. I can protect myself."

Humberto shrugged. "Mr. McGowan already ordered his man Jaeger to stand watch at the front gate. The least Leggy and me can do is keep a lookout over your place."

"I agree." Logan smacked Humberto on the back. "Excellent idea."

"You guys need your sleep, and you—" she jabbed her finger in Logan's direction "—don't need to encourage them."

"We don't need no encouragement, Lana." Leggy lifted his rifle from his side. "We're doin' it."

Logan twisted his head over his shoulder. "I guess it's settled. You've got yourself a couple of bodyguards."

Before Lana could object any further, Humberto and Leggy unfolded the chairs they had slung over their backs, shook out a couple of blankets and made themselves comfortable in front of her house—or as comfortable as they could be with rifles across their laps.

Logan jogged up the steps. "And I'm going to have a look around your house before I leave."

She unlocked her door and pushed it open. "I guess you guys don't think a woman can protect herself."

"The more layers of defense, the better." Logan left her standing by the front door as he checked out all her windows and the sliding door that led from her kitchen to a small patio in the back. He jiggled the handle. "I don't like this."

"It's a sliding glass door with a lock. What's not to like?"

"Someone could cut the glass by the handle and unlock it. Wouldn't even have to smash the window." He crouched down and ran a finger along the track. "Do you have a long piece of wood like a yardstick or something I can wedge in here?"

Her gaze lit on the fireplace tools by the hearth. "I have something better."

She selected a poker from the rack and brought it to Logan. "Will this work?"

"That'll do it." He took the poker from her and inserted it in the door's track, wedging shut the slider. "This way if someone unlocks the door, he still won't be able to slide it open."

"Do you want to check out the bedroom and bathroom, too?"

"Lead the way."

She took him to the short hallway and pointed out the bathroom. "There's just a small window in there. I don't think a grown man or woman could fit through."

Sticking his head into the room, he flicked the light. "That should be okay."

He followed her into the bedroom and checked out the two windows. "Not bad."

"Humberto and Leggy know there's a door and windows in the back, so I'm sure their sentry duty will include a reconnaissance around back."

"I'll remind them on my way out." He squeezed past her, his hand brushing the bedspread on her queen-size bed that would be too small for the two of them. "Are you going to be okay? Helluva day."

She blinked and tossed her hair over one shoulder. "A worse one for Dale…and the kids."

He walked to the front door and she trailed after him, dragging her feet. She'd have to show him out now, even though she'd prefer his company to Humberto's and Leggy's.

As he stepped onto the porch, Logan paused. "One silver lining to all this?"

"Do tell."

"They don't have Gil's journal or they wouldn't be looking for it."

Fifteen minutes later with her guards out front, Lana peeled back the covers on her bed and crawled between the sheets. She mumbled a prayer for Dale's safety, and then curled one arm beneath her head.

She lay staring at the ceiling. Her phone, charging on her nightstand, buzzed once. Her heart fluttered for a second. Maybe Logan couldn't get her out of his head, either, and had texted her a good-night.

She reached for the phone and turned it over. Tapping the message icon, she brought the glowing phone close to her face. A message from Dale popped up, and Lana swallowed against her dry throat as she touched the screen with her fingertip.

The words screamed at her:

Give them the journal or they're going to kill me... and you.

Chapter Five

Logan stretched out across the bed, his boots dangling off the edge, and folded his hands on his stomach as he watched the blinking red light on the smoke detector in the corner of the room.

The men who'd kidnapped Dale McGowan had made a fatal error. They'd lost their element of surprise by snatching the wrong woman. Now Lana, and the people close to her, had a heads-up. Not that he considered himself one of the people close to Lana—although he wanted to be.

Dale McGowan did look like Lana, but even in her picture, Dale lacked Lana's vitality and spark. Having met Lana once, you'd never mistake her identity—or forget her.

Could he forget Lana? He'd have to find a way once he left this town, once he found out everything he needed to know about Major Denver's presence at the embassy outpost in Nigeria. He could at least help Lana reach some closure over her brother's death.

As he sat up and tugged at his first boot, his cell phone rang. His heart rate accelerated when he saw

Lana's number on the display. Had she been thinking about him, too?

"Lana? Is everything okay out there?"

"No. I received a text from Dale's phone. I don't know if the message is really from her or if her captors typed it in for her, but it said if I don't turn over Gil's journal, I'm going to die. They're threatening Dale's life, too." She ended her sentence on a sob.

Logan's fingers curled around the edges of his phone in a tight grip. "Did you notify the police? Are they still at the house?"

"I did not tell the police. Dale, or whoever, warned me not to tell the police or she'd be dead. I can't have that on my conscience. It's already my fault that Dale is in danger."

"It's not your fault." He wiped a hand across his brow. "Did you explain that you didn't have the journal?"

"I tried to tell them that—as much as texting would allow—but I'm not sure they're buying it. I also tried calling Dale's number but nobody answered."

"You can't give them what you don't have, Lana. You need to go to the police and hand over your phone. If Dale's phone is still active, they can triangulate her location."

"If the police come in with lights blazing and sirens wailing, Dale isn't going to make it out alive."

"The people who took Dale are not going to want a bunch of local police or the FBI on their tail over a mistaken kidnapping. They messed up big-time by

snatching Dale and now they're trying to use it to co-
erce you into cooperating with them."

She made a strangled sound across the line.
"They're doing a great job."

"I know you're scared, but think logically. You
have nothing to give them, so you can't save Dale,
anyway. Also, I know it sounds callous, but Dale is
not family. It's not your responsibility to save her—
and they know it. They're not going to gain anything
by harming her…or even threatening to harm her."

She huffed out a breath. "That's not logical at all.
I would save a *stranger* from harm if I could and
Dale's no stranger."

"You just said the magic words—*if you could.* You
can't. You don't have the journal. The best thing you
can do right now is notify the police while Dale's
phone is still hot."

"And if they kill her?"

Logan stood up and paced toward the window of
his hotel room. "They're not going to kill Dale, and
you couldn't stop that even if you wanted to turn over
ten of Gil's journals. You don't have the one they
want. No threats are going to change that."

"All right. I don't know if Jacobs and Zander are
still at the big house, but I'll call the station and let
them know what I have."

"I think that's the best move at this point."

"What should I text back to the kidnappers?"

"What was your most recent response to them?"

"I had just repeated that I don't have any journal."

"Good. Leave it at that, and the next move is theirs."

"I just hope their next move isn't killing Dale."

When Lana ended the call to him to contact the Greenvale police, Logan sat on the edge of the bed with the phone cupped between his hands.

He hoped their next move wasn't killing Lana.

THE FOLLOWING MORNING, Logan grabbed his phone to call Lana when he finished dressing. She'd called him back last night to let him know she contacted the police and they had already started tracking down Dale's cell. She hadn't received any more text messages from Dale's phone and all further attempts to text or call her phone had failed.

After the flurry of texts between Dale's phone and Lana's, Dale's had been turned off.

Now the police wanted to see Lana's phone and those text messages, and Lana wanted Logan to go with her to the station. Whether she wanted to keep him in the loop or she wanted a bodyguard or she felt safe with him—he didn't care. He just wanted to be with her, and he wasn't examining his own motives too closely, either.

Her voice was breathless when she answered on the second ring. "Are you on your way?"

"Just about to leave the hotel. Are you okay?"

"I'm fine. Just cooking the boys some breakfast for their all-night stint in front of my place. They look like hell."

"Keep 'em close if you can until I get there."

"It's daylight. The ranch is busy, and I feel perfectly safe. Oh, and the police are back—a detective,

Detective Delgado, this time who's questioning the kids and Bruce again."

"Can you turn over your phone to him?"

"The police want me to take it to the station. You're sure you don't want me to pick you up at your hotel on my way to the station? That would make more sense than driving back and forth."

"I'm okay with driving back and forth."

"Got it, Tex."

He smiled into the phone as Lana ended the call. Surprisingly, nobody had ever called him Tex before. As corny as it was, he liked it.

He grabbed his jacket from the back of the chair, slid his phone into one pocket and his gun in the other. The idea that someone plotted to kidnap Lana to get Gil's journal filled him with an icy dread. Just because they'd messed up and grabbed the wrong pretty Latina didn't mean they were going to stop.

They'd try again and again until they got the right woman—and that's what he planned to stop. If he and Lana could find Gil's journal and get it into the hands of the right people—people who would investigate the subterfuge going on at that outpost, people who would look into Major Denver's presence there— Lana would be safe and he'd be that much closer to clearing Denver's name.

After last night, the former had become just as important as the latter.

Logan left the city and breezed through the farmlands of the San Joaquin Valley on his way to McG Ranch, no shortage of country music stations on the radio to keep him company. He even spotted a sign for an upcoming rodeo. These areas outside Greenvale took their cowboy culture seriously.

As he hit the last, long, lonely stretch of road to the ranch, he knew he'd made the right decision to come out here and collect Lana for the trip back to the police station. Anything could happen on a road like this.

He made the turnoff to the ranch road, his little rental bouncing and kicking up dust along the way. Had he known when he arrived that Lana lived so far outside the city limits, he would've rented a four-wheel drive.

A hulking presence awaited him at the ranch's front gate, and Logan powered down his window and stuck out his head. "I'm here to see Lana Moreno. I'm a friend of hers."

The man shifted his toothpick from one side of his mouth to the other, took a step back and squinted at the car's license plate. "I got you."

He unhitched the gate and swung it wide.

Lifting his hand, Logan rolled through. At least McGowan had taken some precautions, even though he didn't much like the look of the guy on guard.

He approached the clump of trees that hid Lana's house from view. Those trees probably saved her last night, but he had no doubts that Dale's abductors knew all about Lana's living situation now. Dale McGowan would have self-preservation on her mind instead of Lana's safety, and he couldn't blame her for that. She had two kids waiting at home for her.

Logan parked and jogged up the two steps to the house.

When Lana swung open the door, the scent of maple and bacon wafted from the small kitchen. He inhaled deeply. "Smells like heaven."

"Are you hungry?" She gestured to the two men sitting at her kitchen table. "These two have been trying hard, but they haven't been able to completely finish off everything."

"I wouldn't mind some breakfast." Logan nodded to Humberto and Leggy, who were seated before their empty plates.

As soon as Logan sloughed off his jacket, the two men rose and stretched in unison. Humberto, the more talkative of the two, reached for his hat and coat. "Thanks for breakfast, Lana. We'll be getting back to work now."

Lana flipped a towel over her shoulder and wedged a hand on her hip. "Oh, I see how this is going. The second shift just showed up, so you guys can finally leave."

Looking down, Leggy grinned and nudged the table leg with the toe of his boot. "Nah, we were really hungry."

"Well, I really appreciate it—everything—and if Bruce gives you any trouble about starting work late send him to me."

"Oh, Mr. McGowan's too broken up about Dale's kidnapping to pay much attention to the ranch right now. Right, Leggy?"

Leggy snorted and punched Humberto in the back as they left Lana's house.

"I guess everyone knows about the McGowans' troubles, huh?" Logan pulled out the chair Leggy had just vacated.

"Yeah, and it's more than that." Lana swiped the place mat from the table in front of Logan and replaced it with another. "Humberto is Dale's half brother."

"Keeping it all in the family, I guess." Logan rubbed his hands together as Lana set down a plate loaded with eggs, bacon and potatoes.

"Toast? Coffee?"

"A cup of coffee, please, but I can get it myself." He started to push back his chair from the table.

She pressed a hand on his shoulder. "I'm already up and I need a refill myself."

When she sat down across from him, she put two coffee cups on the table and placed her cell phone next to his plate. "Do you want to see my communication with Dale?"

"Absolutely." He wiped his bacon fingers on a napkin and picked up her phone. "Even if this was Dale typing the messages, they were probably telling her what to text."

Lana's dark eyes grew round over the rim of her coffee cup. "If they were just using her phone to reach me, maybe they had already…hurt her."

"They have no reason to hurt Dale. Her husband doesn't have anything they want—you do. As long as the kidnappers kept their masks in place and Dale can't ID them, she'll be safe. Like I said before, these guys don't want the local police and the FBI coming down on them for a murder they didn't even need to commit."

"Do you think the police can get something from my phone?"

"Not sure." He bit into another piece of bacon, the maple flavor filling his mouth. "You told me they got Dale's number from Bruce and started trying to ping the phone, even before you received the texts."

"I hope they were pinging it while it was still on because it's off now."

"I guess we'll see." Logan finished his breakfast while Lana sipped her coffee.

When he was done, he joined Lana in the kitchen. He bumped her hip with his as they stood in front of the sink. "Let me clean up."

Lana raised one arched brow at him. "You know how to do dishes?"

"Why wouldn't I? I live by myself most of the time. Someone has to do them." He plunged his hands into the warm, soapy water to make his point.

"Most of the time? Do you ever stay at your family's ranch?"

The slick glass nearly slipped from his hands. "You know about my family's ranch?"

Color rushed from her throat to her face. "I—I thought I'd better do a search on you…in case you were an ax murderer or something."

His chest tight, he rinsed out the orange juice glass and held it out to her. "Dishwasher?"

"Everything goes in the dishwasher except the two frying pans, the mixing bowl and the large utensils." She pulled open the door of the dishwasher and took the glass from him. "Your parents' ranch?"

"I'm there sometimes, not on every leave." The fact that Lana had researched him and had found out about the ranch, one of the biggest cattle ranches in Texas, left a bad taste in his mouth. He didn't like people judging him before they got to know him. He scrubbed a pan with the dish sponge. "I'm here now, aren't I?"

Lana opened her mouth and then snapped it shut. She kept her lips pressed into a straight line as she loaded the dishwasher with the dishes he'd scraped and rinsed.

If he poked her, she'd split at the seams. She wanted to ask him something, make some kind of point, but for whatever reason wasn't ready to unload yet. If he knew anything about this woman after being acquainted with her for about twenty-four hours, he knew she'd get around to it sooner or later, but for now he'd take later.

With the kitchen clean and words still unsaid, they put on their jackets and left the house. They stood on the porch while Lana locked up and Logan peered between the branches of the trees that created a semi-circle around her house. When she made a quick turn back toward the door, his pulse ratcheted up a notch.

Had something spooked her?

"Do you mind if we take my truck?" She'd shoved

the key in the lock. "I need to pick up a few things and your car is not going to work."

"Yeah, sure." His heart rate thumped back to normal.

Lana dived back into the house and returned jingling her keys. "Ready."

Logan held the driver's door open for her and then went around to the passenger side, his nerves still jumpy. She hadn't been off the ranch since the kidnapping. He didn't know what awaited her out there.

She put the truck in gear and they bounced along the road to the gate.

The same man who'd been there when Logan drove through hopped off the fence and touched the rim of his hat before swinging the gate wide to accommodate Lana's truck.

She flicked her fingers at the man and then gunned the engine of the truck, which caused the tires to kick up some dust.

A smile played about her lips as she looked in the rearview mirror.

"Not a friend of yours?"

"Jaeger, one of Bruce's most loyal ranch hands—*the* most loyal. He'd do anything for Bruce."

"Including his dirty work?"

"Exactly. How'd you guess?"

"I figured there had to be a good reason why you didn't like the man."

"Lots of 'em."

The truck made one last bounce before hitting the paved road, and Lana straightened the wheel. "I made a call this morning to find out if there were any more boxes coming from Gil."

"Are there?"

"Nobody seemed to know." She flexed her fingers on the steering wheel. "Nobody seems to know much of anything."

Including him. Logan stared at the road in front of them, and then grabbed the dashboard with two hands.

"Lana, slow down. Do you see that up ahead?"

She eased on the brake. "I-it's a person—by the side of the road."

Logan's nostrils flared as his instincts kicked into high gear. Anything unusual now had to be suspect— and a person by the side of the road in the middle of nowhere was suspicious.

"Oh, my God, Logan. It's Dale."

He grasped the door handle. "Slow, slow, slow."

Lana brought the truck to a crawl as they approached the crumpled figure on the road's shoulder. She threw the gearshift into Park and reached for her door.

"Stop, Lana. Don't get out."

"What do you mean? I'm not leaving Dale like roadkill."

"You stay in the truck and keep your head down."

Her head jerked toward him, her dark eyes glassy. "Why?"

"Why did they leave her here? A whole stretch of highway with clear views almost to Greenvale and they dump her off at a curve in the road with a stand of trees. She comes crawling out of the trees precisely when your truck turns up." He put his hand on her arm, vibrating with fear. "Humor me and slump down in your seat. I'll get Dale."

Lana powered back the seat and tipped over to the side, almost flattening herself across the bench seat.

Logan slid out of the truck, his hand on the weapon in his pocket, his heart pounding. He'd been in ambushes before, and this looked like an ambush—with bait and everything.

Hunching forward, he jogged toward Dale McGowan, curled into a fetal position. He kneeled beside her and touched her battered face, once almost as beautiful as Lana's.

"Dale, you're gonna be okay. We're gonna get you out of here."

She peeled open one eye, her lashes caked with blood, and mumbled through her swollen lips. "They're here...and they want Lana."

As the last syllable hung in the air between them, the bullets started to fly.

Chapter Six

At the sound of gunfire, Lana pressed the side of her face against the passenger seat, her fingers digging into the cloth. They were out there, and they meant business.

She covered her head with one arm. They hadn't started shooting into the truck yet, and it was still idling. Had the bullets hit Dale or Logan? A scream gathered in her chest.

They had to be shooting from the left. The right side of the road offered no cover for them. That meant Logan and Dale were exposed.

Lana's feet scrambled, reaching for the brake pedal. Then she reached up and shifted the truck into gear. She eased off the brakes, sending the truck forward in slow speed.

A bullet shattered the driver's-side window, raining glass on her hip and side. She'd gotten out of the way just in time.

The passenger door flew open and Logan shoved a bruised and broken Dale into the cab.

He yelled, "Get out of the line of fire, Lana."

"And put you back in it? No way. Get in the back."

They both jerked as another bullet pinged the side of the vehicle.

"Okay, stay down. Put the truck in Reverse and punch it."

"Not until you get in the back."

"I will." He popped up and fired back at the shooters across the road, which probably explained how he'd been able to keep them at bay.

"Open your back window. I'll guide you." He slammed the door, and the truck dipped as he rolled himself into the back.

Still on her side, Lana eased into Reverse. She hooked her fingers on the bottom of the steering wheel and slid open the back window.

"Gun it!" Logan's voice, clear and strong, carried into the cab.

Lana slid her foot from the brake pedal and slammed on the gas. The truck lurched backward, and Lana held her breath as it almost stalled. Then it roared to life and sped down the road.

Logan shouted steering instructions to her, and she swung the steering wheel right and left to keep on the road.

Several seconds later, the bullets stopped and Lana sat upright. She grabbed the wheel with both hands and continued driving in Reverse until she spied a turnout. She backed into it, spun the wheel around and took off toward the ranch finally going forward.

Dale moaned beside her.

"It's all right, Dale. You're out of danger now."

Dale sucked in a breath. "You're not."

As LANA CAREENED back to the ranch, Jaeger almost wasn't fast enough to get the gates open and she almost plowed through them.

He jumped back and she couldn't even take any pleasure in it.

He must've called Bruce because as they approached the big house, he ran out with the detective close behind him.

Lana squealed to a stop and jumped out of the truck. "It's Dale. We have Dale."

Bruce barreled toward the truck and yanked open the door. "What the hell happened to her?"

Detective Delgado traced his finger around a bullet hole on the driver's-side door. "Did you take gunfire?"

Logan vaulted out of the back of the truck. "It was a trap. They dumped Dale by the side of the road and waited for Lana's truck to come by. Then they opened fire."

Logan swiped at a spot of blood on his cheek and Lana lunged forward. "You've been shot."

"Just a nick from the glass." Logan fished his phone from his front pocket. "Dale needs an ambulance. They beat her."

Lana drove a fisted hand into her stomach as Bruce lifted a limp Dale from the vehicle. Lana said, "She was conscious. She spoke to me."

"She's out now." Detective Delgado crouched beside Bruce, cradling Dale in his arms and whispering in her ear.

Maybe he did still love his wife.

Delgado twisted his head over his shoulder. "What did she say, Lana?"

"Not much to me. Said I was in danger."

Logan ended his 911 call. "She warned me that her abductors were in the area. Probably saved our lives."

"What were they after? Why were they shooting?" Delgado swiped a hand across his creased forehead.

Logan pressed a hand against Lana's lower back. "They were after Lana. She told the officers that last night. They're after her brother's journal. The boy, Daniel, heard them."

"If they were trying to kill Lana, why were they shooting at you and Dale and not her? If she was driving, they would've riddled that truck with bullets."

"I said they were *after* Lana." Logan's hand inched around her waist. "I didn't say they wanted to kill her. If they killed her, they might never get Gil's journal. It might fall into the wrong hands."

Even with her jacket zipped up and Logan's fingers firmly pressed against her hip, Lana shivered. "Shouldn't you have officers at the scene, Detective Delgado?"

"They're on their way. As soon as you crashed through the gate, Jaeger called the house and I sent for patrol cars. Now if you can tell me exactly where this happened, I can direct them where to go."

"It was at mile marker fourteen, just before the curve in the road. They must've been staked out behind the copse of trees in that area. We never saw them…or at least I didn't."

Logan raised his hand. "I returned gunfire, kept

them at bay. I didn't make out anyone except a few heads popping up."

Delgado scratched his jaw. "Do you think you hit anyone?"

"I don't know. Is there a problem if I did?"

"Do you have a conceal-carry permit for the State of California?"

"I'm Delta Force, sir. I think I know what I'm doing, permit or not."

"I can look the other way—for now."

About thirty minutes later the sirens announced the ambulance before its arrival, and the EMTs got to work on Dale.

"Thank God the kids are in school." Bruce hovered over the stretcher, running his hands through his hair. "Is she okay? Is she going to be okay?"

"You can follow us to the hospital, sir." The EMTs loaded Dale into the back of the ambulance and it took off with Bruce's Mercedes right behind it.

"When are you going to question her?" Logan picked something out of Lana's hair and held out his palm to show her a piece of glass. "You're okay?"

"I'm fine." Physically she'd escaped the attack unscathed, but emotionally? She had people ready to abduct her for a journal she didn't have. Total basket case.

Delgado coughed. "We're going to question Dale at the hospital as soon as she's ready, but we need to question you, too, Lana. This all has something to do with Gil's death?"

"I believe it does."

"I know he was killed on duty in Nigeria. I'm sorry."

"Thank you." She dipped her head. "I never believed for a minute the government's account of what happened. I've been trying to get some clarity…some truth. I always believed Gil's journal held the key to that truth, and now I'm sure of it."

"The text message you got from Dale's phone last night referenced the journal."

"That's right." She ticked her finger between her and Logan. "We were on our way to deliver my phone to the police when we spotted Dale—and all hell broke loose."

"We'll still need your phone, maybe now more than ever. If these people have come to Greenvale and are endangering our citizens' lives, we're going to put a stop to it, no matter who they are." Delgado jerked his thumb at Logan. "Is he involved?"

"No." Logan pinched Lana's side. "Just a friend here for a visit."

"Lana needs friends like you right now. We're a small department. We can't assign an officer to guard Lana, but we can give you both an escort back to town if you want it."

"Oh, we want it." Lana nodded. "Can you let me know if Dale tells you anything useful, like who I need to look for over my shoulder?"

"We'll keep you posted, and I'll have one of the officers at the scene of the shooting come down here when he's done to accompany you back to town." Delgado secured his hat back on his head. "In the meantime, I'm going to head to the hospital to see if I can talk to Dale."

Logan tipped his head toward the entrance to the ranch. "Do you know if Jaeger's still at the gate."

"According to Bruce, Jaeger will be there until he picks up the kids from school in a few hours."

"They're going to be so relieved when they learn their mother is safe." *At least someone's safe.* Lana shoved her hands in her pockets and hunched her shoulders.

As if reading her mind, Logan put an arm around her shoulders. The weight of the pressure made her feel secure, locked down.

When Delgado drove away, Logan turned to her. "Do you want to take the truck back to the gate and wait there for the patrol car?"

"I do."

"Are you okay to drive?"

She held one hand in front of her, steady and sure. "I am now. Thanks for holding them off. Thanks for rescuing Dale."

"I think you were the hero of the hour, driving your truck like that between us and the gunfire. You were crazy to do it, but you probably saved our lives."

When they reached the driver's-side door of the truck, Lana ran her fingers over the bullet hole in the door. "What do you think they were planning?"

"I think they wanted to get me out of the way and kidnap you in Dale's place." He opened the door for her and kicked some glass from the running board with his foot.

"Did you see Dale's face? They must not have believed her when she told them they had the wrong woman, and that was their way of showing their disbelief. What are they going to do when they have their hands on the *right* woman?"

Logan took her by the shoulders and pressed a hard kiss against her mouth. "That's not going to happen, Lana. They're not going to get to you as long as I'm in the picture."

Her lips tingling, she said, "Then I hope you're in the picture for a long time."

The ride back to town proved to be uneventful. The patrol car followed them all the way to the police station, its lights on a slow roll.

When they walked into the station, a Detective Samuels led them to an interrogation room where Lana handed over her cell phone.

"Have you heard anything from Detective Delgado yet about Dale McGowan?"

Samuels scrolled through the messages from Dale's phone and took some notes. "She's okay and out of immediate danger. Apparently, her abductors kept her blindfolded, so she didn't get a look at them. Had no idea where they took her, either. They sedated her, so she can't even tell us how long they traveled in the van."

"The van?"

"She knows it was a van because of the way the door rolled open and the long bench seat in the back. That's also when they sedated her."

Lana covered her mouth with one hand. "I'm so sorry that happened to her."

"And you think it's because someone is after your brother's journal?" Samuels held up her phone.

"Yes."

"Do you have the journal?"

"No. I expected it to be among Gil's possessions in the box the marines sent me, but it wasn't there. I thought it might've been stolen when I didn't see it, but judging the actions of these people they're still looking for it, too."

"Why do you think they want it?"

Lana's gaze darted to Logan's face. "I think it's because I've been questioning what happened at the embassy outpost Gil and the other marines were guarding. The government has an official explanation, and that's the one they want to stick with."

Samuels drew a square on the table around her phone. "Are you trying to tell me you think the United States Government is behind the kidnapping and beating of Dale McGowan?"

"Maybe not the government." Lana folded her hands on the table and twisted the rings on her fingers. "But it could be someone within the government in an unofficial capacity."

"If this is truly what's going on—" Samuels drove his finger into the table "—this is something we'll have to hand off to the FBI. We'll do our regular police work and try to track down Dale's kidnappers and the people who shot at you, but we'll have to leave it up to the prosecutor to determine a motive."

"I can help them out with a motive. I know this is what's going on. I'm just sorry Dale got roped into it."

"It's because the two of you look so much alike— or at least you used to." After a few more questions, Samuels snatched up the phone again. "We'll be doing some forensic work on this to see if we can pin down a location. We'll have to hold on to it."

"I understand."

"In the meantime—" Samuels's gaze darted from her face to Logan's "—be careful."

"She will... I'll make sure of it." Logan pushed back from the table and extended his hand to Samuels.

Once outside, Lana blew out a long breath. "Do you think I should contact the FBI on my own? Cordova?"

"I think you should get out of town."

She tripped over a crack in the sidewalk, and Logan caught her arm. She couldn't even walk without Logan saving her.

"You're kidding."

"What are you going to do here, continually look over your shoulder for who knows what? You heard the detective. Dale can't ID her abductors. If you don't know who they are, how are you going to recognize the danger when it's staring you in the face?"

"I can't just pick up and leave. I told you that. I have—" she waved her arms around like a crazy person "—responsibilities."

"You don't think Bruce will let you off?" He lunged in front of her to get the door of the truck, the bullet hole in the side causing her heart rate to spike. "I think his wife's appearance sobered him up, gave him a different perspective."

"He *did* seem rattled, but that has nothing to do with me. I have things to do at the ranch, horses to exercise and train…other stuff to do."

"I think he's going to understand that you want to get away—for your safety. He can make other arrangements, at least until you get Gil's journal and turn it over to the proper authorities. Once that happens, you should be out of danger."

She zipped her lip on arguing with Logan. He'd never understand financial obligations like hers. He'd been born with a silver spoon in his mouth, or at least silver spurs on his boots. And she had no intention of telling him about her other obligation here.

She climbed into the truck and slammed the door on his handsome, pampered face.

Undeterred, Logan slid into the passenger seat and continued, "But until that happens…"

She cranked on the engine and revved it. "You act like finding Gil's journal is a done deal. I have no idea where it is. I expected it to be among his things—in that box. When it wasn't, I figured it was stolen. According to Dale's kidnappers, it wasn't."

"Let's take another look in the box." He snapped on his seat belt, dropping his campaign to get her to leave her job, her life, her everything at the McG Ranch.

She punched the accelerator of the truck as tears pricked her eyes. If her everything really was at McG, she was in big trouble.

She'd been in big trouble for a while.

She sniffed. "I went through everything in the box. I even searched the pockets of Gil's clothing. It's not there."

"What if it's not a journal?"

"What do you mean? It's a journal. I told you about Gil's journaling. He always kept one with him."

"I mean, what if it's not a physical journal? You're looking for a book, probably about yay big." He held his hands about six inches apart. "Leather-bound or cloth-bound, little pen stuck in the side. Maybe it's in a different format."

Lana skimmed her hands over the steering wheel, a bubble of excitement filling her chest. "It could be in a different format because he wanted to hide it."

"Exactly." Logan snapped his fingers. "Let's find it."

Lana glanced at her rearview mirror and eyed the patrol car following at a discreet distance, the only thing keeping her within the speed limit. He trailed them right up to the gates of the ranch until Jaeger let them through.

Lana called out the window. "Any more news about Dale?"

Jaeger tipped his hat back on his head. "She's out of danger, but she'll be spending the night for observation."

"And the kids?"

"Safe and sound with Dale's mother in the house." Jaeger smiled with a twist of his lips, turning the smile into a smirk. "Safe and sound."

Lana dropped her head once in acknowledgment and sped down the road to her house.

"What is it with that guy?"

"Jaeger? I don't know. He's generally unpleasant. He's Bruce's confidant, which gives him a sense of superiority."

"As long as he keeps an eye on that gate and is as unpleasant to strangers as he is to you."

She'd figured out long ago that Jaeger knew everything Bruce knew, which meant he knew all her secrets, too. But right now, Gil's secrets were more important than hers.

Lana parked the truck and Logan followed her into the house.

He dragged the box of Gil's things from the corner to the front of the couch and then sat down, patting the cushion beside him. "Did you find any flash drives or computer disks among his belongings?"

"None." She lifted a coffee mug from the box and pressed it against her cheek.

"You said you communicated with him online. Did he have a laptop with him?"

"Not his own. He used the computers at the compound. I doubt he would've put anything personal on those."

Logan plucked a toiletry bag from the box and unzipped it. "Books?"

"Lots of those." She pushed some items aside as she reached into the bottom of the box to pull out a stack of several books. "Gil liked to read, mostly sci-fi and fantasy."

"You went through those already? Shook them out?"

"You mean like there might be a book within the book?"

"Something like that—a smaller pamphlet shoved inside."

Lana collected all the books and dropped three in Logan's lap and lined up the remaining four on the coffee table. She grabbed the edges of the first book's cover, splayed the book open and shook the pages.

Logan did the same with his books, but nothing fell out of any of the books, and no hollowed-out insides provided any surprises.

"It sounded promising." Slumping back against the couch, Logan thumbed through one of the books. His brow furrowed and he sat up straight, clutching the book with both hands.

Goose bumps rippled across her flesh. "What is it?"

He flipped through the book, stopping every few pages to jab his finger at the margins. "Did Gil always make notes in books when he read?"

"Notes? These are fantasy and sci-fi books, not Shakespeare." She scooted closer to Logan, her thigh pressing against his. "What do you see?"

He flattened the book on his lap and skimmed the tip of his finger down a page, reading the margin note and then flipping to another page to read another note. "'Making tamales after Luisa's graduation. Bobby crashing Ricardo's bike. The pink blanket with kittens.' Does any of that mean anything to you?"

Lana put a hand to her throat when Logan read the

last note, the heat rising from her chest scorching her fingertips. "L-Luisa and Bobby are two of our siblings. These are events from our lives. Why did he write those things throughout the book?"

Logan held up the book and shook it. "Lana, this is it. This is Gil's journal—and he's written it in code— a code only you would understand."

Chapter Seven

"Oh, my God. That's totally something Gil would do." Lana grabbed a book she'd discarded earlier and started to flip through the pages. "He's written more notes in this book, too, almost like a personal history—but I don't know what he means. I don't understand this."

"It's all right." Logan smoothed a hand down Lana's rigid back as if to soothe an agitated cat. "We'll figure it out, but I think I'm right. Why else would he write random things like this in the margin of a book?"

"I don't know." Lana jumped up and wandered to the window. "Why would he expect me to catch onto this?"

Logan paged through the rest of the books while Lana paced the room. "Five books. He's written in five of the books—the same kinds of notes in all."

"Why would he do that?"

"For exactly the reasons we've seen—to hide his journal. If he'd kept a regular journal, it would've been long gone by now. Even if he'd written in the books without using code, someone could've discovered that."

"Why did he put this on me?"

Logan dumped the books on the table and met Lana on her next trip around the room. He grabbed her trembling hands. "He probably did it for himself, Lana. He didn't know he was going to die at that outpost. He wrote it in this code for himself, to protect himself and to protect the information he gathered. The fact that he masked it in terms that only a family member might understand was just further protection."

"Me, not any other family member—just me."

Logan cocked his head. How could she know that? Then he shrugged. "He was closest to you, right?"

"We were the two afterthoughts. Our other siblings are much older."

"I didn't realize you two had other siblings."

"Four."

"What?"

"Four more. Gil and I have four older siblings."

"Wow. Well, he chose you and the method is brilliant."

"So brilliant, I don't have a clue how to solve it." She pulled her hands away from his and covered her face. "I'm going to fail him all over again, just like everyone else failed him—the marines for sending him there, the government for its secrecy, our congressman, even the military who was close enough to render aid and didn't. You know there were units who could've helped but were never sent in?"

"I—I heard that." Logan's eye twitched. "We're not going to fail him this time, Lana. We'll figure it out. All we need is a start, some verification that this is real. Then we might be able to turn it over to people who break codes for a living. They could decipher the rest."

"Can't they do it now?" She split her fingers and peered at him through the cracks. "Can't we just turn these books over to the code breakers and have them figure it out?"

"We would need some proof first. Then they'd need your help for the rest. They would need to understand what the events mean—only you know that."

"If this is all true, the people after this journal wouldn't understand it even if they got their hands on it, even if they could crack the code. Am I right?"

He leveled a finger at her. "They'd need you."

"Oh, Lord." She spun around and made a beeline for the kitchen. "Is it too early for a drink?"

As she swung open the fridge door, Logan returned to Gil's fantasy books and stacked them back in the box. "We'll have to make copies of these pages or scan them. These books can't be the only record of Gil's journal. If someone breaks in here and steals this box, we have nothing—even if they don't know what they have."

Lana returned carrying two bottles of beer. "I think we deserve these after what we've been through today."

"Cheers." He clinked the long neck of his bottle with hers and took a gulp of beer. "What's the best way to get a copy? We could take a picture of each page with your phone. That would be easier than scanning each one."

"Your phone. Mine's been confiscated."

"True." He pulled his phone from his pocket. "We should start right away. I don't want this slipping through our hands."

"We don't even know where to start. Which book contains the beginning of the journal? What order are they in?"

"That's not important right now. We need to preserve the pages, duplicate them. We can always rearrange them later."

"Do you want to get started now?"

"I suppose so." He lifted an eyebrow in her direction. "Do you want to start working on the code now?"

"I'd love to, but I told you I don't have the slightest idea what it all means." She scooped up the books from the box and carried them to the kitchen table.

He joined her and grabbed the book on the top of the pile. "Let's start working on this methodically. Do you have a spiral notebook or a legal pad?"

"I think I can dig one up. Why?"

"You can start by going through each book and writing Gil's phrases in order, at least from each book. Then start looking for connections or patterns—months the events occurred, any special meaning associated with them, and so on. Codes are usually based on numbers. Does that make sense?"

"I guess so. You'll be taking pictures of the pages in one book while I go through the pages of another?"

"Teamwork." He held out his fist for a bump and she touched her knuckles to his.

As Logan flattened out one of the books on the table, she went in search of a notebook. She found one in a desk drawer under a pile of odds and ends and brought it into the living room, where she sat cross-legged on the couch with one of Gil's books.

A smile touched her lips as she scribbled the nonsensical clues onto the pad of paper. Gil had recorded some of the silliest moments of their childhood, moments she would be sure to remember because they'd discussed them enough times over the years.

Their hardscrabble childhood in Salinas hadn't been all bad, but they'd spent so many years dealing with the effects of Dad's alcoholism. Sibling after sibling had escaped the too-small clapboard house with the dripping faucets and the faulty water heater until only she and Gil had remained. Even Mom had bolted in the end, using *abuelita's* illness as an excuse to leave the husband who was never able to lift her out of poverty.

Finally, Dad had gotten sober and had taken the job with his old friend, McGowan. She'd followed him here later—it had been inevitable.

"Those notes must mean something to you."

"What?" She jerked up her head and rubbed her eyes.

"I've been watching you for the past several minutes, and a whole range of emotions just played across your face." He dropped his voice and almost whispered. "But it all seemed to end on a sad note."

"Sad?" She twisted her hair around her hand. "It all just makes me think about Gil. We have to do this for him, Logan. And for Major Denver."

"I agree." He held up the book he'd been photographing. "One down, four to go. Anything strike you?"

She stretched out her legs and wiggled her toes. "Just the realization that my whole life has been a series of one haphazard event after another—no actions on my part, just reactions."

Logan turned his chair to face her and hunched forward, resting his elbows on his knees. "Maybe you should forget all this, Lana."

"Forget?" She ran her fingertip along Gil's words. "I can't forget about Gil."

"I'm not saying you forget your brother, but let him rest in peace. Don't pursue this anymore. I'll handle it. You go and make some different choices in your life starting now, choices based on what you want."

"It's funny, but for the first time in a long time that's exactly what I am doing. This—" she held up the notebook "—is my choice."

"Then we'll carry on." He reached for the ceiling and yawned. "I could use some food before attacking the next book, though. Are you hungry? We haven't eaten since breakfast."

"My stomach just growled, so I guess there's my answer." She swept the book and the memories from her lap and pushed up from the couch. "Unless you want breakfast again, I don't have much in the way of food to cook."

"I can eat breakfast at any time of the day. I suppose calling for a pizza out here isn't going to work."

"Nearest pizza place won't deliver to the ranch—too far." Lana snapped her fingers. "I have an idea. Jaeger mentioned that Dale's mother was watching the kids. I can beg some food from her."

"Do you know Dale well?"

She turned away from Logan and bent over the couch, gathering her notes. "Yeah, I do."

"Why the drinking problem? Did that start after she married Bruce?"

"It did. I'm not making excuses for her, but it can't be easy being married to that guy."

"No kidding. Cute kids though."

Lana pasted a smile on her face and spun around. "Yes, they are. I'm so glad they're safe."

"So, how does one go about begging food from Dale's mother? What's her name?"

"Alma. Alma Garcia."

"How do we hit up Alma?"

"Since the police have my phone and I don't know Alma's number by heart, we'll have to walk over to the ranch and make our case."

Logan put his hands together and raised his eyes to the ceiling. "I'm good at begging."

"Hummph." She grabbed her jacket from the back of a kitchen chair. "You've probably never begged for anything a day in your life."

He dropped his gaze, meeting hers, and his nostrils flared. "Don't be so quick to judge, Lana."

"You're right. Sorry." She swung open the door

and a cool blast hit her hot cheeks. "I'll let you do the begging."

As they walked to the big house, Logan asked, "Do you think Bruce will be back from the hospital?"

"I don't know. I'd never seen him as rattled as he was when he took Dale out of my truck."

"Maybe he finally realized his wife didn't set up her own abduction to score a weekend away."

"Maybe he did." Lana climbed the two steps to the McGowan front door and rang the doorbell.

Alma opened the door, a frown already creasing her brow, giving her the same worried look she always had whenever she encountered Lana. "*Hola, Lana. Qué pasó?*"

"Nothing happened, nothing's wrong, Alma, except for Dale being in the hospital." She gestured to Logan. "This is my friend, Logan Hess. Logan, Alma Garcia."

"Ma'am, nice to meet you." Logan took Alma's hand and laid on the Texas charm. "Everything's fine except my stomach is rumbling something fierce."

Lana put a hand over her mouth and rolled her eyes, but Alma proved to be no match for Logan's wiles.

"Oh, you poor boy. You don't go to Lana's house when you're hungry."

"*Abuela?*" Carla had crept down the stairs and now hung on the banister at the bottom, her big, dark eyes wide until they focused on the two people on the porch. Her face broke into a smile. "Hi, Lana. They found Mama."

"I know, sweetie, and she's going to be just fine."

Alma's body stiffened. "Carla, did you finish your homework?"

"Almost. Can I stay down here with Lana and her friend?"

Alma shot a quick glance at Lana. "Of course. I'm just going to get them some leftovers."

"Ah, you're an angel." Logan pressed a hand over his heart.

"Follow me." Alma crooked her finger. "No Mexican food, but I made pasta tonight and there's plenty left over. Dale is still in the hospital and Bruce is with her."

"How is she?" Lana put her hand on Alma's arm while smoothing Carla's hair back from her forehead.

"She's fine, no permanent damage. She's coming home tomorrow and then…" Alma trailed off as she opened the door of the large fridge.

"Then I'm sure Bruce will keep her safe." Lana dragged a stool up to the large butcher-block island in the center of the kitchen, and then pulled Carla between her legs as she started fixing her ponytail.

Logan wedged a hip against the island, pointing to the containers in Alma's hands. "Do you need some help?"

"No, thank you." She stacked the plastic containers on the counter. "I'm going to give you everything. I already fed Humberto and his sidekick."

"We don't need all of that, Alma."

"Speak for yourself." Logan rubbed his hands together.

Lana punched Logan's rock-solid bicep, which almost broke her hand. She shook it out. "Won't Bruce need something to eat when he comes home tonight? There are enough leftovers here to feed the family tomorrow night, too."

Alma waved one set of stubby fingers at her. "Bruce is staying at the hospital with Dale tonight. He's a changed man, Lana, really, and Dale, too. You'll see."

"I'm sure they are." Lana wrapped Carla's ponytail around her hand. "How about you, Carla? Are you okay? That must've been so scary for you, and I know you stepped up to protect your brother."

Carla twisted her head around and a sweet smile touched her lips. "It was scary, Lana, but now that Mama is back, it's okay."

"You're right. It is." Lana wrapped her arms around Carla and kissed the soft indentation of her temple. "Now you'd better do as your *abuela* says and finish that homework."

She begged for two cookies from her grandmother and then scooted out of the kitchen and up the stairs.

"She's a good girl." Alma shook out a plastic bag and started to put the containers inside.

Logan grabbed the next one from her hand. "I'll do this. I really appreciate it."

Placing her hands on her ample hips, Alma tilted her head. "Lana doesn't cook much, but she could learn. I could teach her."

"Thanks, Alma. I'm good."

Alma wagged her finger in her face. "You know the way to a man's heart is through his stomach."

A tingling flush crept up Lana's chest, and she raised her hand to stop any more embarrassments coming out of Alma's mouth.

Too late.

"Lana needs a good man. A man of her own." Alma jabbed Logan in the side. "A man and a family of her own."

"Oh, God, Alma. Logan is not that kind of friend."

"He should be, eh?" Alma narrowed her eyes, assessing Logan from head to toe.

When Logan's face displayed a red tinge, Lana decided it was time to leave. "I think this is the price we have to pay for the food."

"I don't think it's too high." Logan peered into the bag loaded with Alma's leftovers and sniffed.

Lana hopped from the stool and gave Alma a one-armed hug. "Thanks for the food…and the advice. I'm fine."

When they got back to her house, Lana popped the lids of the containers. "Lasagna, fettucine alfredo, salad and some garlic bread. I hope you're hungry."

"I am. You heat up the pasta in the microwave, and I'll serve the salad in a couple of bowls and stick the bread in the oven."

Standing in front of her fridge, surveying the pathetic contents, Lana said, "I wish I had some red wine, but all I have are a few more beers."

"That's fine." Logan reached past her to pluck a

bottle of salad dressing from the door of the fridge. "Why is Alma so anxious to see you married off?"

She hunched her shoulders. "Just an older woman looking out for a younger one—in her own way."

"I didn't realize you were so close to Dale's family."

"Dale and her family were the first people Dad met when he moved here." The microwave beeped and Lana retrieved the containers, steam rising from the cracks in the lid. "Pasta is ready."

During dinner, Lana steered the conversation away from Dale and the kids and the ranch and even Gil's journal. Instead, she peppered Logan with questions about Major Denver and what he and his Delta Force teammates had discovered so far—and she got an earful.

"So, the powers that be already know the initial emails implicating Denver were fake, they know that he didn't kill that Army Ranger or push his Delta Force teammate off a cliff and they know he wasn't responsible for the bombing at the Syrian refugee camp. And they *still* believe he's a traitor intent on compromising U.S. security?"

"I don't think the army believes it, but the investigation has reached different levels, levels involving the CIA and covert ops."

Lana carefully dragged the tines of her fork through some tomato sauce on her plate. "Do you think those agencies might know more about Denver and his activities than you do?"

"They might, but they might also be interpreting

those activities incorrectly. I think the major was onto something, and he was working with some inside sources. Someone wanted to put a stop to that—and him."

"I don't doubt it, not after what Gil told me about the situation at the embassy outpost." She stacked their empty plates and bowls. "You wash and I'll load the dishwasher? Then we can get back to the journal... unless you want to get back to your hotel."

"I think I can get through another couple of books. How about you?"

"If I stick to writing out the events and not thinking about each one." She swept the dishes from the table and carried them to the sink.

"You're going to have to start analyzing them at some point so if it slows you down in the initial process, that's okay." He joined her at the sink and pulled down the door of the dishwasher.

They cleaned up together, and Lana tried not to get sucked in by the comfortable domesticity of the situation. Logan was here to get enough info from her regarding Gil's coded journal, and then he'd take it and give it to the proper authorities. She'd have to content herself with getting to the truth of Gil's death—that's all she'd ever wanted, anyway—until she met Logan Hess. Now she wanted more.

"Back to work." Logan squeezed out the dish sponge beneath the water and grabbed a towel for his hands. "Ready?"

"Yes. Absolutely. Work."

This time they worked across the room from each

other, but the sense of companionable teamwork continued. Occasionally, Logan would break the silence to ask her if she needed something or to check on her well-being.

She couldn't tell if he was truly concerned for her or if he just wanted her to work harder. She didn't want to view his actions through rose-colored glasses as she'd done for others before him. She was older and wiser now, not a silly schoolgirl.

A knock on the front door made her jump, one of Gil's books sliding to the floor.

"I'll get it." Logan closed the book he was working on, using his phone for a bookmark. He strode past her and twitched the curtains to the side. "It's Humberto and Leggy."

"Oh, my God, am I going to have to make them breakfast again tomorrow?" She scrambled to her feet and peered through the window, waving.

Logan opened the door on the two men waiting on the porch. "Are you here for guard duty?"

"Last we heard, the police haven't caught the guys who kidnapped Dale." Humberto stomped his boots on the porch. "So, we're in again."

Lana put a fist on her hip. "Didn't Jaeger recruit more guys to patrol the front gate?"

"Yeah, but that's the front gate, not back here." Humberto jerked his thumb over his shoulder. "We have our chairs and everything."

Leggy nodded and spit to the side. "Chairs and everything."

"You really don't have to put yourselves out. I have

my own gun, and I can protect myself, especially with the extra security at the entrance to the ranch." She nudged Logan's arm. "Tell them, Logan."

"You boys did a great job last night, but it's my turn tonight."

Lana whipped her head around. "Don't be ridiculous. You have a hotel room in town. In fact, you should be heading back to that hotel room about now."

Humberto backed off the porch. "We got you, boss. She's all yours tonight."

"All yours." Leggy winked before following Humberto off the porch.

Her blood sizzling, Lana slammed the door. "What is wrong with you?"

"Me? Nothing." Logan's eyebrows jumped to his hairline.

"They're going to think—" she flicked her fingers at the door "—you're sleeping in my bed."

"Did I imply that my sentry duties would take place in your bed?"

Stalking away from him, she threw her arms out to the side. "*My turn tonight.* What do you think they thought? That was a smirk on Humberto's face. I know him, and he was smirking."

"I didn't see a smirk. I don't think they got the wrong impression at all—and if they did?"

"If they did?" She tripped to a stop and snatched a pillow from the couch, throwing it at him. "I don't want people thinking I sleep around. I just met you. I barely know you. You're not sleeping in my bed."

Logan's eyes popped and his mouth gaped open for

a second. "What's wrong with you? Did I *say* I was sleeping in your bed? I'm sleeping on the couch, keeping one eye on the door and my gun by my side. I'm only trying to protect you, Lana. I'm sorry if I gave Humberto and Leggy the wrong idea. If they know you, they already know you don't sleep around."

Lana took a deep breath and folded her arms across her stomach. Everything was just too close to the surface tonight—being with Carla and Alma, Gil's family memories.

She wanted Logan here. Had been dreading the moment when he grabbed his jacket and walked out the door. Even though she'd caught a spark from his eyes a few times, he'd been nothing but gentlemanly to her and she knew she could trust him to sleep on her couch.

Putting her hands to her hot cheeks, she said, "I'm sorry. It's just that there's a small-town mentality here, and I don't like to be the subject of gossip."

"Understandable." He snatched the pillow from the floor where it had landed at his feet. "I shouldn't have sprung that on you in front of those two. The later it got, the more I started thinking that it would be a good idea for me to bunk on your couch. Guess I should've run it by you first."

"Probably."

"If you'd like me to leave, I can grab those two and station them back in front of your house." He held the pillow in front of his face.

A laugh bubbled up from her chest. "I'm sorry I threw the pillow at you. You're welcome to stay on my couch, and I appreciate your concern. But I do think I'm safe on the ranch now. The kidnappers blew it by taking Dale, didn't they?"

"Showed their hand for sure, but you're not out of danger, Lana. I'm sure Dale told them you lived here, and you can't blame her."

"After getting a look at Dale's face, I don't blame her for anything." A cold shiver snaked up her spine, and she hunched her shoulders. "Since you're going to be taking over my couch, I'll get this stuff out of the way. I'm almost done writing Gil's notes from the third book. We can pick it up again tomorrow."

"Let's call it a night. I only ask for a toothbrush."

"You're in luck. I have a stockpile of them from my dentist. I use an electric." She made a notation in Gil's book where she'd left off and gathered the notebook, sticky notes and pens. She placed her work beside Logan's on the kitchen table.

Tapping the book on the top of the pile, she said, "I hope we're on the right track."

"I think we are." He pointed to the cleared-off couch. "Blanket and pillow?"

"Coming right up." She ducked down the short hallway and raided one of the cupboards for a blanket, fresh towel and toothbrush. "I don't have an extra pillow."

"That's all right." He held up the one she'd tossed at him. "I can use this one. It can double as a weapon."

She gave him a half smile as she placed the folded blanket and towel on one end of the couch. She flicked the toothbrush in his direction. "This, too."

He caught it with one hand. "Thanks. Who needs a gun?"

"I do, and mine's beside my bed, so don't make any sudden moves in the night."

"Wouldn't think of it." He drew a cross over his heart with the tip of his finger.

Thirty minutes later, snug in her bed—alone—Lana could hear the TV from the other room. Was Logan having trouble sleeping, too? It couldn't be the same reason that kept her tossing and turning. She'd made it clear to him that she didn't want him in her bed.

At least not now...

THE FOLLOWING MORNING, Lana tiptoed into the living room and squinted at Logan sprawled on her couch still sleeping. It had been a long time since she'd had a man in her house, and he seemed to overpower her small space.

She crept into the kitchen, turning on the lights beneath the cabinets, and ran some water for coffee. The noise caused Logan to stir.

"You don't have to creep around in there. I'm awake."

"You could've fooled me."

"I'm a light sleeper." He sat up and the blanket fell from his torso, revealing his bare chest.

Lana turned away and stubbed her toe. "C-coffee?"

"Yes, please. Alma was wrong about you. You can whip up a mean breakfast."

"Thanks, but I don't pay any attention to Alma's advice."

Someone knocked on the front door, and Lana cranked her head over her shoulder. "I'll get it. You should get that stuff off the couch."

"Wouldn't it be better if I left it here as proof I slept on the couch?" He folded the blanket and smoothed his hands over it.

"I think it would be better if you put some clothes on." Lana scurried into the living room and peeked through the curtains. "Oh, my God. It's Dale."

Logan took a step toward Lana and she waved him back. "Grab that blanket and get dressed."

Once Logan left the room, Lana threw open the front door. "Dale, what are you doing here? You should be resting."

Dale pushed past Lana and limped into the living room. "I just wanted you to hear it from me first, Lana."

"Hear what?" Lana knotted her fingers in front of her.

"Bruce and I are taking the kids away for a while— just for everyone's safety. I swear to you, this attack has sobered us up—literally, in my case. I'm going to be a better mother, Lana. I promise you that. I'm going to take better care of Carla."

Logan cleared his throat as he returned to the room. "I'm glad you've recovered so quickly, Dale, and it's probably not a bad idea to take the kids and lay low for a while, but what do you have to prove to Lana?"

Dale's dark eyes widened as she took in Logan.

"I—I—I'm sorry, Lana. I didn't realize you had company."

"It's all right. I'm tired of keeping the secret from him, anyway." Lana closed her eyes and blew out a long breath. "Logan, Carla's my daughter."

Chapter Eight

The woman who could be Lana's sister backed up to the front door, one hand over her heart. "I'm sorry. I'll talk to you later, Lana. A-and thank you for saving me on the side of the road, Logan."

When the door closed behind Dale, Lana opened her eyes and swept a tongue across her lower lip. "You didn't guess that Carla was mine?"

Had he? Were the signs there? Lana had kept talking about her obligations and responsibilities, her reluctance or inability to leave the McG Ranch. All her excuses had rung hollow with him—until now.

But a daughter? Carla?

"I didn't know." Lifting his shoulders, he spread his hands in front of him. "I'm sorry."

"You don't have any reason to apologize."

"Why didn't you tell me?" He drilled the heel of his hand against his forehead. "Wait, Bruce doesn't know?"

"Oh, Bruce knows...now."

Logan's stomach lurched. "Is Carla his? Yours and Bruce's?"

"God, no." Lana charged toward the kitchen and ripped open a packet of coffee. She dumped it into the filter and turned to face him, wedging her hands against the counter behind her. "I made a stupid mistake when I was a teenager, and Carla is the result of that mistake."

"You turned her over to Dale and Bruce?"

"I was just seventeen and had no means to raise a child. Dale and Bruce had been married a few years and couldn't conceive. When they finally did, Dale had a miscarriage. She was afraid to tell Bruce, afraid he'd divorce her."

"Dale passed your baby off as her own?"

"Alma and my father cooked up the plan between them. My father had already been out here for a few years and knew the Garcia family. When my mother called to tell him I was pregnant, he figured this was the solution to everyone's problems."

Probably just the beginning of Lana's.

"You moved to Greenvale to give birth and then handed your child over to Dale?"

"Yes." A tear glistened on the end of her lashes and she swiped it away. "I did it to appease my family."

"How did Bruce not figure that out?"

"Bruce was out of the country for a few months. He didn't suspect a thing. Came home to his wife and newborn daughter."

"But the truth came out."

"Doesn't it always?"

Her lips twisted—along with his heart.

"Did you stay here after giving up Carla?" He took

a step toward her, but she folded her arms in front of her in a defensive move.

"Not at first. I left, did some traveling. But Mom was in Mexico, Dad had to quit his job at the ranch and I had a strong desire to see the daughter I'd abandoned when she was two weeks old." This time a tear escaped and crawled down her face.

"You didn't abandon Carla. You left her with an established couple, a grandmother, a grandfather, financial security and stability."

Rolling her eyes, she ran one finger beneath her bottom lashes. "Stable? You've seen Bruce and Dale in action."

"At seventeen, you couldn't have known anything about their marriage. You did the best you could, not to mention you had adults you trusted giving you advice." He shoved his hands in his pockets. "What about the father?"

Lana's eyes flew to his face. "Ah, not available."

"Did you tell him about Carla?" He couldn't help the surge of jealousy that almost strangled him.

"I did." She plucked at the hem of her T-shirt. "Not available."

Whatever that meant. But she didn't want to reveal any more, and he didn't want to push her.

"That's what you meant about responsibilities and obligations. You stay here for Carla."

"It's my excuse, anyway. Alma would never let any harm come to those kids, Bruce, either, believe it or not."

"How did Bruce come to find out Carla wasn't his biological child?"

She screwed up her mouth to one side. "You know, how these things usually come out—a drunken argument between the two of them. Dale threw it in his face."

"He must've been livid to be tricked like that." Logan clenched his jaw. He actually had sympathy for Bruce.

"He was fit to be tied at first, but he loved Carla. He even loved Dale, and it gave him some leverage with me."

"Is that why he torments you?" The newfound sympathy for Bruce evaporated like mist. "He uses Carla to keep you around?"

"I guess you could say that. It's not like I want to leave." She turned back to the coffee maker. "Not really."

In two steps he crossed the kitchen and touched her stiff shoulder, whether she wanted him close or not. "Isn't it hard for you to see your daughter every day with another family, another mother?"

"It's not easy, but I've enjoyed watching her grow— sort of like her guardian angel."

"And now she's leaving." He squeezed her shoulder. "You should, too."

"She'll be back."

"Maybe this is your chance, Lana. Dale came over here for a reason this morning. Just out of the hospital and hurting, she wanted you to know she planned to change. Maybe Dale wants a chance, too—the chance to be Carla's mother without her bio mother looking over her shoulder and judging her."

"Ha! I'm hardly one to judge." She held up the coffeepot. "It's ready."

He straddled a stool at the counter. "I still want to talk to Dale, don't you?"

"A-about Carla?" The hand pouring the coffee jerked and the stream of liquid splashed on the countertop.

"About the kidnapping." Why would talking to Dale about Carla make her nervous? Lana had already acknowledged the child was hers.

"Oh, yeah, of course. Sorry." She wiped up the coffee spill. "My mind's still on Carla."

"I can understand that." He cocked his head as he took the coffee cup from her. "Did you ever think about trying to get her back?"

"I'd never do that to Dale. Even though she hasn't been the best mom in the world, she loves her kids." She reached back to get her own cup and settled across the counter from him.

"Is Daniel hers? Hers and Bruce's?"

"He is. As often happens with couples, once they... adopted Carla, they had an easier time getting pregnant the next time and Dale made sure to take care of herself."

"She didn't take care of herself during her first pregnancy?"

Lana shook her head. "She was drinking. That's probably why she had the miscarriage."

"No wonder she wanted to hide that from Bruce."

He swirled the coffee in his cup, his gaze tracking the circles. "Did you know at the time why Dale miscarried?"

"No, but I'm not patting myself on the back just because I didn't know what had happened. Even if I had known, I'm pretty sure I would've succumbed to the pressure to give up Carla. I had nobody on my side."

"That must've been hard on you, Lana." In fact, Lana had seemed to have a rough road all her life. The urge to rescue her from all of it burned deep in his chest, but he recognized that feeling for what it was, and the last time he'd given in to it things hadn't worked out too well—for him, anyway. "The father…"

She blinked and smiled brightly. "Breakfast?"

"Maybe just some eggs and toast. I can handle that." He reached across the counter and snatched a lock of hair from her messy ponytail. "Why don't you get dressed, and then see if Dale is willing to talk to us?"

"I'm sure she is." She flicked her fingers at the cupboards. "Do you think you can find everything?"

"I'll rummage around."

She took her coffee with her as she left the kitchen.

Banging around the cupboards and drawers, he located a frying pan, spatula and bowl. He may have exaggerated his bachelor skills to Lana, but he could handle scrambled eggs and toast.

As he beat the eggs and milk with a fork, he heard the shower from the bathroom and the sound was enough to fire up his imagination about Lana and her petite but curvy body. She'd made it clear last night she had no interest in bedding him but now that he knew she'd gotten pregnant as a teenager, he understood her desire to keep her reputation shiny and clean here at the ranch.

That didn't mean she was celibate——did it? He hoped to hell not because he had every intention of getting to know that woman better, of gaining her trust.

The butter sizzling on the stove jarred him out of his daydream, and he dumped his eggs in the pan.

By the time Lana emerged from the back, he had two plates of only slightly browned scrambled eggs ready to go with some sliced and buttered toast tucked next to them. He'd found grapefruit juice in the fridge and had poured out two glasses.

Lana's damp, wavy hair snaked down her back as her bare feet slapped against the tile floor. She grabbed the fridge handle and said over her shoulder, "This looks perfect. Thanks."

"Liar." He pointed to the ketchup she had in one hand and the salsa in the other. "If it looked so perfect, you wouldn't be scrambling for condiments to make it better."

"These?" She hoisted them in the air and winked. "I eat everything with salsa."

After breakfast, Lana cleaned up the kitchen while he hit the shower. He could've waited until he got back to his hotel, but at the rate they were going through Gil's books that might not be for a while.

They'd probably be dropping in on the McGowans, too, and he didn't want to look like a slob.

If he was going to be the one on Lana's side, he wanted to look worthy of the part. Why hadn't Carla's father helped Lana? Thinking about the father of Lana's child caused his blood to percolate in his veins. Did she want to protect him for some reason? He didn't deserve it, but he was probably a dumb kid who'd been afraid of telling his parents he'd gotten a girl pregnant.

Logan did his best with the female toiletries available to him in the bathroom and finished off by brushing his teeth. When he returned to the living room, Lana had claimed the end of the couch again, book spread open in her lap.

She looked up and rubbed her chin. "You could've used one of my disposable razors for that scruff—not that it doesn't look…okay."

"As long as it looks…okay, I'll wait to use my own stuff at the hotel. Did you talk to Dale yet?"

"I called the landline at the house. She'll call us when Bruce leaves to do some errands to get ready for their trip. It's always easier to talk when Bruce isn't there."

"I thought he was a changed man and they were ready to start a new life together." Logan grabbed his phone charging on the kitchen counter and got his camera ready for another round of pictures.

"Baby steps. You can't expect Bruce to leap into a new persona."

"What's his problem with you, anyway? Did he

start harassing you after he found out you'd given birth to Carla?"

Her lashes fluttered as she returned her gaze to the book open in her lap. "Pretty much."

"Because he was angry at you for being in on the scheme? For not telling him?"

"Worse." She flattened her hands against the pages of the book and drew back her shoulders. "I always kept to myself when I came back here to live with my father. Bruce had always fancied himself a ladies' man and thought he could crook his little finger at any woman and she'd come running. He crooked at me, and I didn't."

"That ticked him off."

"It did, and then when he found out about Carla and realized I wasn't as pure as I pretended to be, the torment started."

"What an ass that guy is." He formed his hand into a fist. "I could clock him for you if you want."

Pursing her lips, she tilted her head. "That would be a very bad idea, and you know it."

"Yeah, but the satisfaction." He drove his fist into his palm where it landed with a smack.

"It would be short-lived—until your arrest for assault and battery and probably court martial."

They worked in silence until the phone on the wall in the kitchen jangled.

Logan dropped his cell. "I almost forgot you had a landline in here."

"Sometimes the cell reception falls off, so I keep it *in case* of emergency, and it's an emergency now because the cops have my phone." She jumped up from the couch on the second ring and grabbed the receiver.

"Uh-huh. Okay. We'll be over in about fifteen minutes." She hung up the phone. "That, in case you didn't figure it out, was Dale. Bruce just left and the kids are at school."

"What are the kids going to do for school when they leave? It's not even close to summer break."

Logan had just finished photographing the pages of the fourth book, which he closed and stacked on the other two. Lana had the third on the couch, and he grabbed that, too, along with her notes. "I'm going to put these back in the box. Now we just have one left."

"Good idea. I'm not sure what Carla and Daniel are going to do about school. Should I even ask, or would I seem too much like a hovering bio mom?"

"Ouch. Did I say that? What do I know, anyway? Ask away."

Lana left him again to finish getting ready, which by the sound of it involved drying her hair and, by the look of it when she returned, putting on some makeup. She looked pretty without a scrap of makeup on, but a little went a long way on her already-striking features. Even in a pair of faded jeans and a denim work shirt, Lana took his breath away.

"Sorry." She grabbed her jacket. "I always feel like I have to put on my face with Dale."

"So you don't get taken advantage of again?"

"Maybe that's it."

They stepped outside and she locked the door behind them.

Logan nodded at Jaeger, who must've been on one of his patrols of the ranch.

The grim man touched two fingers to his forehead. "Be careful now, Lana."

She tipped her head and kept walking, her boots crunching against the ground.

Logan put a hand on her back. "Why is that guy always lurking around?"

"He's Bruce's right-hand man, grew up with him. Bruce gave him a job when he got out of prison."

"Prison? What for?"

"Stalking and battery."

"That's the kind of guy Bruce wants around his family?"

"Like I said, Jaeger is as loyal as the day is long. He'd never do anything to hurt Bruce or his family."

"Yeah, but what about you and others?"

"He's been behaving himself ever since he was released. His ex-wife moved far, far away and changed her name. I think she was his obsession and he doesn't pose a danger to anyone else."

Logan snorted. "Ringing endorsement."

When they reached the big house, Dale swung open the front door before they even had a chance to ring the bell. "C'mon in. I don't know what I can tell you though."

"How are you feeling, Dale?" Lana tapped her temple. "That looks like a nasty bruise."

"I'm doing okay even though I have to drink through a straw. I got a few painkillers from the doc."

She held up one hand. "I know what you're thinking, but I'm off the booze."

"I hope it lasts." Lana pulled at Logan's sleeve. "I know you two didn't formally meet by the side of the road when you were dodging bullets or this morning when you barged in, but Dale this is Logan Hess, Logan, Dale McGowan."

Dale sized him up with her dark eyes as her hand lay limply in his grasp. "I got your name from the cops at the hospital. Said you saved my life."

Logan dropped her hand and put his arm around Lana's shoulders. "I think we both have Lana to thank for that. If she hadn't moved the truck into the line of fire, we both might be dead."

"That's our Lana—brave and self-sacrificing as always."

Logan opened his mouth and Lana bumped him with her hip. "Are you up to answering a few questions about your abductors? I know you probably spoke to the police about all this at the hospital, but since it concerns me I'd like to hear it straight from you."

"Sure, I can talk about it." Dale clapped her hands. "Rosa, refreshments, please."

A middle-aged Latina scurried into the room. "What would you like, Mrs. McGowan?"

Lana waved. "Hi, Rosa. How's Manuel and the kids? How's Jamie doing at Berkeley?"

"She's fine, Miss Lana, majoring in political science. What would you and your friend like? Coffee? Iced tea?"

Dale rolled her eyes. "Just bring us *something*, Rosa. This isn't a restaurant."

Lana winked at the housekeeper. "Coffee would be great and some of Alma's coffee cake if you have any."

Logan had watched the entire exchange through narrowed eyes. It told him everything he needed to know about Dale and Lana. Dale might be able to offer Carla all the material comforts of life, but Lana would've been the better mother to the girl—hands down.

Dale reclined on the couch, smoothing her hands over the silky material of her dressing gown. "Now, what do you want to know about those SOBs who grabbed me and beat me up?"

"I suppose you weren't able to identify them? Detective Delgado said they were wearing masks when they invaded the house and kept you blindfolded and drugged."

"That's exactly right." Dale's long fingernails dug into the material she'd been stroking before. "They burst in here with ski masks covering their faces, made some ridiculous demands and then tied something over my eyes and dragged me from the house. All I could think about was Carla and Daniel."

Logan coughed. "They asked you about a journal?"

"They kept screaming in my face about it. I tried to tell them I didn't know what they were talking about." Dale pinched the bridge of her nose and closed her eyes. "Once they got me into the back of the van, they put a cloth over my nose and mouth and knocked me out. When I came to, I was inside a building, but I had no way to identify the place. I already told the detectives that."

Lana scooted up to the edge of her seat and planted her hands on her knees. "When did you realize your abductors had mistaken you for me?"

"When they started asking me about my brother and what he had told me about the embassy."

As Rosa maneuvered back into the room carrying a tray loaded with cups and plates, Dale put a finger to her lips, made plumper by the swelling from her injuries.

Logan jumped from his chair and took the tray from the small woman. "I'll get this, thanks."

Rosa's gaze darted to Dale's face and then back to Logan. "Thank you, *señor*. Anything else, Mrs. McGowan?"

"No, thank you, Rosa."

Since Dale seemed disinclined to move even her pinkie finger, Lana took it upon herself to stir some cream and sugar into a cup of coffee and hand it to her hostess.

Logan reached for the tray on the coffee table and nabbed a piece of coffee cake. He broke off a piece and pointed it at Dale. "You set them straight, right? Told them you weren't Lana Moreno. Told them Lana Moreno lived in a back house on your property. Told them Lana Moreno received a delivery from her deceased brother, Gilbert."

Dale's hand jerked with the coffee cup midway to

her lips, and the brown liquid sloshed over the side and dribbled onto her white dressing gown. "What did you expect me to do? Do you see my face? They didn't stop with my face. They punched me in the stomach. They held a knife to my throat."

Lana clicked her tongue. "I wouldn't expect you to die to protect my identity, Dale. You did what you had to do, and Logan knows that."

"I'm sorry, but in a way you can thank me for sparing you, Lana. If they hadn't grabbed me first, they would've been on the hunt for you." She pulled the plunging neckline of her robe up to her chin. "And you don't want those guys finding you. I meant what I said when Logan rescued me roadside—my captors will kill you if they have to. They're dangerous…and that's why we decided to take the kids and relocate for a while."

"Where are you going?" Lana brushed the crumbs from the coffee cake from her fingers into her plate.

"We'd rather not tell you—just in case. We're hiring a nanny and a tutor to come with us, so Carla… the kids will be well cared for and will be able to keep up with school."

"That's not a bad idea." Logan leveled his finger at Lana. "And you should do the same, Lana. Get away from the ranch. I'm sure Bruce will understand. Right, Dale?"

Dale batted her long lashes at him in a futile attempt at flirtation. "Yes, of course. I'll talk to Bruce. You aren't teaching any lessons now, anyway, and we're not buying any more new horses for the time being. In fact, there hasn't been a lot for you to do on the ranch for a while, Lana. And with the kids gone…"

"Leave the ranch? I have no idea where I'd go." Lana stacked up the empty plates on the tray and crumpled a napkin in her fist. "I can't just take off for parts unknown."

"You did that once before, didn't you?" Dale snapped her fingers. "Oh, yes, that's when you had a little money, isn't it?"

Lana stood up suddenly, bumping her knees against the tray. "I just ask that you bring the kids to my place so I can say goodbye."

"Of course."

The doorbell rang deep in the house and Dale swung her legs from the couch. "I'll get that and walk you out at the same time."

Logan wedged himself between Dale and the front door to peer through the peephole. "It's a really built guy with blond hair and a tight white T-shirt."

"That's Lars. He's my massage therapist." Dale placed her hands on Logan's hips to nudge him aside. "I'm expecting him."

She opened the door with a flourish and threw herself at the young, pumped-up man, giving him a kiss on the cheek. "I'm so glad you could come on such short notice, Lars. You heard what happened? I'm going to need some tender handling."

"Of course, Dale. You're going to feel like a new woman." He nodded to Logan and Lana as he brushed past them to set up the table he carried in a case.

"Lars has heavenly hands." Dale raised her eyes to the ceiling as if thanking the heavens for those hands. "I will let you know before we leave, Lana. Take care of yourself."

"Take care of the kids, Dale."

"We will, changed woman and all that." Dale grabbed Lana's sleeve and tugged as she jerked her head toward Lars. "This could've all been yours, too, Lana if you'd played your cards right."

Lana broke away from Dale and stumbled onto the porch.

Logan steadied her with a hand on her back. "What did Dale mean by that?"

"Just Dale being Dale." Lana straightened her spine, shrugging off his hand. "I wonder if she's really going to change her ways. I don't think Bruce would be too happy to see massage-boy in there doing his thing."

"I guess that's between them. I meant what I said in there about leaving the ranch, Lana. You're not going to be safe here, especially with the family gone from the front house."

"And I told you...and Dale, I have nowhere else to go and no money to get me there."

She stomped off toward her house and despite her petite size, Logan had to lengthen his stride to keep up with her.

"I might have an idea...or two."

"I'm not sure I want to hear your ideas." She clumped up the wooden porch of her house and shoved the key in her dead bolt. She froze and stepped back, leaving the key chain in the door.

"What's wrong?"

"I locked that dead bolt when we left."

A spike of adrenaline flooded his system, and his muscles coiled. "What about the lock on the door handle?"

He answered his own question by reaching forward and twisting the handle. "That's still locked."

"Because it locks from the inside, too. The dead bolt does not."

"Step back." He hooked a finger in the belt loop of her jeans and pulled her back, tucking her behind him.

He pulled his gun out of his jacket with his right hand and slid the key out of the unlocked dead bolt with his left. He inserted the key into the door handle and turned.

As the door cracked open, he kicked it with his foot. It swung wide and he stepped across the threshold, leading with his weapon.

Lana's neat house had been tossed, ransacked from top to bottom.

Before he could stop her, Lana darted past him and dropped to her knees next to Gil's box. She twisted her head over her shoulder, her face completely drained of color.

She didn't even have to say the words, he knew what was coming out of her mouth next.

"It's gone—all of it. Gil's journal, my notes, all gone."

Chapter Nine

"Stay right there." Logan charged past her and checked every door and window in the house.

He returned, his chest heaving and his face grim. "There's no sign of a break-in. Nobody tampered with the locks on the front door. How did they get in?"

"Does that matter?" Lana gripped the sides of the cardboard box, what was left of Gil's life scrambled inside. "They took the books. They took my notes."

"They didn't take my phone." Logan placed his gun on the kitchen table within easy reach. "And more importantly, they didn't take you. They're not going to know what to make of that code. Not even an experienced code breaker can figure that out without input from you first. You are the key to Gil's code."

She held on to the box even tighter, the edges cutting into her palms. "That does not make me feel good. In fact, that makes me feel sick to my stomach."

"What makes me feel sick to my stomach is the fact that someone waltzed right onto this property, right up to your house and somehow got inside without raising an alarm—all under the watchful eye of Jaeger, who saw us leave."

Jerking her head to the side, she said, "What are you implying?"

"I'm not implying anything." Logan smacked his hand on the counter next to his gun. "I'm saying Jaeger, or someone with his approval, allowed Dale's kidnappers back onto this property and into your home."

"Why would he do that?" She sat back on her heels, still not willing to release the box containing Gil's possessions.

"I have my suspicions, but I'm going to find out for sure since Jaeger's lurking around your house right now." Logan strode across the room and threw open the front door. "Jaeger, where are you going so fast?"

Lana scrambled to her feet and came up behind Logan on the porch. She peered around his broad back at Jaeger, his head cranked over his shoulder, his thin face pale.

He spit into the dirt as he turned slowly to face Logan. "Whaddya want?"

"Why'd you let Dale's kidnappers back on this property? Bruce isn't going to be too happy when we tell him."

A thin smile stretched Jaeger's mouth as he hunched his shoulders. "Don't know what you're talkin' about, buddy."

Logan launched himself off the porch, advancing on Jaeger, who took a step back. "He ordered you to do it, didn't he? You don't make a move without the boss's approval, do you? Why'd he do it?"

"You're crazy." Jaeger's hands curled into fists at his side. "If you're trying to impress Lana, don't bother. That girl don't give it up for nobody. Gave it up easy enough to some rich boy back in Salinas ten years ago, but hasn't opened her legs since."

White-hot anger whipped through Lana's veins but before she could even open her mouth, Logan flew at Jaeger and the sickening sound of flesh pounding flesh thudded through the air.

Jaeger staggered back, his nose spouting blood, but like a bowling pin he swayed forward and threw a punch at Logan. With lightning speed, Logan shifted to the side while swinging his left fist up and making contact with Jaeger's chin.

Jaeger choked and made a dive at Logan's midsection, wrapping his arms around Logan's body, throwing all his weight against him to take him down.

Logan kneed Jaeger in the groin and as he doubled over, releasing his opponent, Logan linked his hands and brought them down on Jaeger's back like a sledgehammer. Jaeger collapsed to his knees, his hands clutching his stomach.

"You bastard. I'll kill you."

Jaeger scrambled in the dirt, reaching for Logan's legs, but Logan retaliated by kicking the other man in the chest.

"That's enough, Jaeger. Stop." Bruce charged forward and grabbed a handful of Jaeger's shirt, dragging him back—not that the broken and bloody man posed any kind of threat to Logan, who stood over him, his fists still clenched, Jaeger's blood on the sleeve of his shirt.

Lana skipped down the steps and hooked her fingers through Logan's belt loops. "Did you hurt your hand?"

"A little." Logan shook out the reddened fingers of his right hand. "Why did you allow your wife's abductors back on the ranch, McGowan? You should've called the police instead. Are you stupid?"

Bruce shoved a handkerchief at Jaeger and shook his head at his condition. "I didn't do any such thing, Hess. You're lucky I'm not going to call the police right now—on you for assaulting my employee."

"Your…employee—" Logan kicked his boot in Jaeger's direction "—let those men into Lana's house. They stole her brother's journal. They could've done worse."

"Oh, is Gil's journal gone, Lana? I thought you didn't have it."

"You know damned well it is. That's what you planned all along, isn't it?" Standing beside Logan filled her with strength, and she pulled back her shoulders. "You made some kind of deal with those men to let them have what they wanted—men who kidnapped your wife, terrorized your children."

"You and your friend live in some kind of fantasy world." Bruce gave Jaeger a shove in front of him. "I don't know what you're talking about. If someone broke into your house, I can have the locks changed before Dale and I leave. You know we're leaving, don't you? You brought danger to our home, to my wife, to *my* children."

Lana snorted. "You and your wife brought danger to those kids every day with your behavior."

"We've given Carla a lot more than you ever could—and you know it. If you want to keep living in this sweet setup, keep seeing your daughter every day, you're going to have to find yourself a better class of friends." Bruce nodded toward Logan.

Logan's muscles tensed, and Lana ran a hand down his back as if calming a stallion. "He's not worth it, Logan."

"I'll tell you what, girl. We both know there's not much work for you do to with the horses, but when Dale and I come back we can look into having you help out Rosa at the house."

Jaeger guffawed through his broken nose, and Bruce smacked him on the back as they turned and walked back to the big house.

Logan growled, "I can have another go at him if you like."

"Don't bother." She trailed her fingers along the veins standing out from his forearm and could feel the rage pulsing there. "Besides, if he thought he could insult me with that comment about working alongside Rosa, he's way off the mark. Rosa is worth twenty of him *and* his wife put together."

"He invited those men back onto his property to give them Gil's journal and get rid of them." Logan curled his bruised hand into a fist.

"In a way, you can't blame him." She pulled at

Logan's arm. "Let's go inside, and I'll get you some ice for that hand."

"Can't blame him? Is this whole ranch crazy?"

"Bruce gave them an opportunity to find the journal so they'd leave and not bother him or his family again—or me, come to think of it." She finally got Logan inside the house and slammed the door behind them.

"If he knew how to reach them—and I wonder how he did—why not just call the cops on them and have them arrested for assaulting his wife?"

"Jaeger has a lot of contacts with the underbelly in this town. It wouldn't surprise me at all if he sent out feelers to contact these guys. Bruce figured, give them what they want and get them off the ranch." She patted a cushion on the couch. "Sit."

Holding his wrist, Logan sank to the couch. "But you and I both know that's not the end of it. They're gonna need you eventually, Lana."

"Well, Bruce doesn't know that…or doesn't care once he has his family off the ranch." She put a glass beneath the ice dispenser on the front of the fridge and filled it to the top. Then she dumped the ice in a plastic bag, and wet down a cloth.

Logan eyed her as she returned to the living room. "I can't believe you're making excuses for his behavior when he put your life in danger."

"I'm not making excuses for him." She extended her hand and wiggled her fingers. "Let me see that hand, Tex."

He flexed his fingers and held his hand out to her. "It sure sounds like you're letting him off the hook."

With the damp cloth, she dabbed the droplets of Jaeger's blood staining his hand. Then she rubbed at the sleeve of his shirt. "If you get this off right now and soak it, that blood will probably come out."

Logan unbuttoned his shirt and sloughed it off his shoulders. "It was dirty, anyway."

Lana snatched it from him, her gaze greedily wandering across the white T-shirt stretched across his chest. "Thanks for standing up for my honor, by the way."

"I despise guys like Jaeger."

Logan clenched his jaw and Lana figured he had a million questions about what Jaeger said and about Carla's father. Maybe she'd tell him that story one day—if they had more days together.

She held up the bag of ice. "Put this on your hand while I dunk this shirt in some soap and cold water."

"Yes, ma'am."

Draping the shirt over her arm, she walked into the kitchen. As she filled the sink with cold water, she leaned toward her reflection in the window to study her bright eyes and flushed cheeks. The excitement of the fight still thrummed through her veins, and the fact that Logan had done it for her made her heart swell.

She placed a wet hand on her chest. This heart had been in danger ever since she laid eyes on the tips of Logan's black cowboy boots. She hadn't felt so susceptible to a man's charms since Carla's father had pinned her with his baby blues. But when push came to shove, Blaine's armor had been made of tin and his promises proved as hollow as a papier-mâché piñata.

She added a little soap to the water and scrubbed at the bloodstains once or twice before leaving the shirt to soak.

When she returned to the living room, Logan was pacing the floor, the ice pack discarded on the coffee table.

"Come back here." Lana crooked her finger at Logan. "You landed a couple of solid punches, and that hand needs ice."

Logan perched on the edge of a stool at the counter that separated the kitchen from the living room and doubled as her dinner table most nights. "You really need to get out of here, Lana."

"And I told you, I have no place else to go." Shaking the bag of ice in front of her, she strolled toward him. "Hand."

He flattened his hand on the counter, his knuckles already red. "I have an idea, a place where you can go."

"I'm not going to Mexico." She settled the ice pack on his hand and patted it into place. "Do you want some ibuprofen to go along with that?"

"Texas."

"What?" She turned from the cupboard where she'd been retrieving a glass. "I'm not going to Texas."

"It's perfect. Think about it." He patted the phone in his pocket. "We can work on the journal together. I have four out of the five books right here, and you can start re-creating your notes. More importantly, you'll be safe, away from this ranch where others are so quick to sell you out."

"The ranch?" She widened her eyes. "At first I thought you meant Texas, as in your place, but you want to bring me to your family's ranch? You're just going to show up on their doorstep with a stranger?"

"I wouldn't want my family to know what you were doing there, so you could come there under false pretenses."

"That's even worse. Crashing at someone's home while lying to them?" She snatched the glass from the shelf and filled it with water. Shoving it in front of Logan along with a tablet of ibuprofen, she said, "You probably need something stronger than ibuprofen if you think I'm going to do that, because you're loco."

"What's the big deal?" He caught the ice pack as it slipped from his hand and readjusted it. "My family's ranch is huge, the house is huge and the people there are not going to notice another…employee."

"Employee?" She hunched over and planted her elbows on the counter, burying her chin in one palm.

Did she expect him to smuggle her onto the ranch as his girlfriend? Maybe he already had a girlfriend there. He hadn't copped to a wife and children, but he didn't say anything about a significant other.

"You train horses. We have horses." He curled his fingers and inspected his knuckles. "Lots of horses."

A flutter of hope stirred in her chest, and she coughed. "If the ranch has lots of horses, I'm sure it already has lots of horse trainers."

"We do, but the woman who was giving riding lessons to kids is pregnant and taking a break. My parents were just talking about that before I went on my leave—and then there's that."

"What?" She studied his perfect face framed by his thick, light brown hair—a look straight out of central casting for the heroic young cowboy who saves the day.

"My parents weren't expecting to see me this time and they'll gladly accept anyone I bring with me."

"Oh, that's comforting." She straightened up from the counter and brushed her hand across the tiles. "They'll welcome any stray you drag along with you?"

"Why interpret it that way?" He shoved the ice aside and pointed a finger at her. "You have a chip on your shoulder."

"No, I don't." Gil used to tell her the same thing and hearing it from the lips of another man she admired caused a knot to form in her stomach. "I'd feel out of place, like an intruder."

"You'd be coming as my guest."

"Correction." She held up one finger. "Employee."

"How about a combination of the two? I don't want anyone to question why I'm bringing a…friend to the ranch. I don't want anyone to know what we're working on, but a friend who also trains horses and can pick up Charlotte's lessons? That would work and not raise any suspicions."

"I'm not going to Texas, Logan."

"You can bring your own salsa."

Her mouth quirked into a smile. "Even that's not enough to lure me."

"What would be?"

His green eyes seemed to smolder, and a tingling sensation crept through all the right parts of her body—or the wrong ones.

She spun away from him and swung open the door of the refrigerator, burying her head inside. "Nothing's going to lure me, Logan."

"Money?"

"What?" The pleasurable tingles she'd been enjoying bubbled into anger, and she slammed the fridge door, rattling the condiments.

He splayed his hands on the counter. "Money? I mean for giving lessons. I know you send everything you earn to your mother, so if money would help, we can offer you a good salary for the lessons. It's not like it's charity or anything like that."

"No, thank you." Why did everyone think she could just be bought off? She must be giving out some kind of vibe. "Do you want to take Alma's leftovers back to the hotel with you for lunch?"

"I'm sorry if I offended, Lana. You keep saying you can't leave the ranch and your job. I'm just trying to make it easier for you to do that."

"Leftovers?"

"No, thanks." He slipped off the stool. "I'll get some lunch when I get back to town. Do you need any help cleaning up? They did a number on your place."

"Nope. It looks like they found what they wanted

pretty quickly." She waved a hand at the box, as tears stung her nose.

She'd lost Gil's books, Carla was leaving and now Logan would leave. Everyone left, eventually.

"You're sure?" Logan took a step toward her, raising his hand and then dropping it.

"I'm sure."

"Before I leave, I'm going to have a talk with Humberto and Leggy about keeping an eye on you."

"You're going to get them in trouble with Bruce."

Logan squared his shoulders. "Bruce is already in trouble with me. He allowed the men who beat up his wife access to your house. He can now spare a couple of his guys to make sure those men don't come back."

"I'm sure Humberto and Leggy already heard what happened and have their own plans."

"I knew I liked those guys." Logan grabbed his jacket and flexed his fingers. "Thanks for the ice. It helped."

"Keep it up when you get to the hotel."

"Lana—" he shrugged into his jacket "—we're still going to work on the journal together, right? Even if you don't come to Texas?"

"Of course." She couldn't let him go that easily. "Maybe you can print out those pages from your phone and I can go through them again and write out the events. It should go faster this time."

"Good. Maybe we can start up again at my hotel when you bring me my shirt."

She covered her mouth with one hand. "I forgot about your shirt."

"That's fine. Leave it. The longer it soaks the greater the chance I can get rid of Jaeger's blood, right?"

"Probably." She sprang forward and got the door for him. "Thanks for everything today. Thanks for being here and…sticking up for me against Jaeger."

"It's about time someone stuck up for you, Lana Moreno." He walked outside and waved from the porch.

She shut the door and locked it. "Get a grip, girl. You're going to see him again. It's not like he's disappearing forever—not yet."

She swooped through the living room, closing drawers, straightening pillows and restacking books. Had they made it into the bedroom? She hadn't even checked.

She stood at her bedroom door, holding on to the doorjamb on either side. They'd tossed a few drawers and rummaged through her closet but must've realized early on that the books in the box, along with her notepad, contained Gil's account of his time at the outpost.

They should've never left the box unsecured, but who would've thought Jaeger would be letting Dale's abductors back onto the ranch?

Once she put her bedroom back together, she stepped into the bathroom, where they hadn't bothered to disturb anything.

Her boot kicked something on the floor and she glanced down, head cocked. Hadn't disturbed anything except her lipstick, apparently.

She crouched down and snatched the tube from the floor, feeling behind the toilet for the lid. Then she stood up and faced the sink.

Gasping, she stepped back as she read the words scrawled in pink lipstick across her mirror.

Not done with you, Lana.

Chapter Ten

Logan shook Humberto's hand. "Thanks, man. With dirtbags like Jaeger around, Lana needs all the protection she can get."

Logan trudged back to his rental car, parked on the other side of the trees that blocked Lana's house.

Why had she been so prickly about going to Texas with him? It solved a lot of her immediate problems. The money comment really set her off. He knew it had been a mistake as soon as the words left his mouth, but he still couldn't figure out why. If she came to his family's ranch as a horse trainer and picked up Charlotte's lessons, why wouldn't she get paid for that?

He never claimed to understand women any better than the next guy, but Lana was like the Rubik's Cube of women.

As he walked past her house, the screen door banged and flew open.

Lana charged down the two steps of the porch and changed course when she spotted him. She rushed at him, hair flying behind her, and he dug the heels of his boots in the dirt to prepare for the impact.

As Lana launched herself at him, he wrapped his arms around her. "What happened? What's wrong?"

She tilted back her head and her eyes looked like dark pools of fear. "I'm coming to Texas."

"Why? What's going on, Lana?" He stroked her hair. As much as he wanted to believe she'd changed her mind based on his well-reasoned proposal, the panic coming off her in waves suggested another reason.

"In the house." She turned and pointed. "A message. They left a message for me on the bathroom mirror."

His arms tightened around her. "How the hell did I miss that when I went in there?"

"They didn't touch the bathroom, otherwise. You wouldn't have noticed unless you stood at the sink right in front of the mirror."

"What did the message say?"

"D-do you want to come back inside and look?"

"Lead the way."

She took his hand and half dragged him back to the house, as if afraid the message would disappear.

He followed her into the bathroom and faced the mirror with its lipstick message. "They know already, Lana. They know they can't figure out Gil's code without you. I could kill Bruce for letting them at you."

Dark eyes met green ones in the mirror. "The message made me realize I'm not safe here, Logan. Not Humberto and Leggy, not my gun, not even you can keep me safe at this ranch. Now that you humiliated

Jaeger, there's no telling what he might do with Bruce gone. He could set me up just to get back at us. He thrashed a woman within an inch of her life before, and that was someone he professed to love. He's not going to show me any mercy."

Logan took his fist and smeared the words on the mirror. "Then we're Texas-bound."

THE DOUBLE H RANCH, Hugh Hess for Logan's grandfather, father and brother, put the McG to shame. Lana tried not to let her mouth drop open as Logan's brother drove across their land, which had to have a house somewhere amidst all the acreage.

Hugh rested his hand on the top of the steering wheel and pointed to the right. "The horses are out that way, Lana. It sure was a stroke of luck when Logan ran into you. We were in danger of losing some of Charlotte's students when she went on maternity leave."

"I'm surprised you bother giving riding lessons on a ranch this size."

Logan, sitting behind her in the Jeep, poked her arm where it rested on the center console.

"We've always done so. We have folks coming in from Dallas and Fort Worth to get lessons and ride. It's a tradition for us and people have come to expect it of the Double H." Hugh waved out the window at a couple of men repairing a fence.

"Thanks for giving me a chance on such short notice."

"A recommendation from my brother is good

enough for us." Hugh adjusted his rearview mirror. "You've known each other long?"

"Not long at all." Logan hunched forward in his seat. "I told you, Hugh. Lana is the sister of a friend. I heard she needed work, knew about Charlotte and thought this would be a solution for everyone."

"It is." Hugh nudged Lana's shoulder. "Just thought Logan might be using the employee angle to bring in one of his girlfriends."

Lana swallowed. "Oh? Has he done that before?"

Hugh's gaze darted to the mirror as Logan punched the back of his headrest. "You'll have to ask him about that."

"There's Charlotte's house." Logan rapped on the back window. "A lot of the ranch hands live beyond it down that road."

Lana peered out the window at the neat cottage. "Was Charlotte living there full-time? Will she mind a stranger moving in?"

"Charlotte and her husband live in Fort Worth. He's a software engineer. Charlotte would use the house on and off, nothing permanent. She won't mind. All the furniture and household items belong to the ranch." Hugh swung the Jeep to the left and rolled up in front of the house. "Home sweet home—for now."

Lana stepped out of the car while Logan circled to the back to get her bags. "You can go ahead, Hugh. I'll get Lana settled, and then I'll bring her up to the house. I'm assuming the old man wants to meet her?"

"Of course." Hugh winked at Lana. "Our father

likes to think he still runs the place and wants to know everything that goes on."

"That's understandable." She cupped a hand over her eyes and turned toward a large, rambling house in the distance. "That's the family house?"

"Yep. Mom and Pop live there along with me and my wife, Angie, and our two kids, and our other brother, Cody, and his wife and their daughter." He clapped Logan on the shoulder. "Only Logan went his own way to do his Delta Force thing."

"Delta Force thing." Logan snorted and balanced her smaller bag on top of her suitcase. "Why don't you head on up."

"Welcome to the Double H, Lana." Hugh tipped his white hat and climbed back into the Jeep.

Lana waved her hand in front of her face at the dust kicked up by his tires.

Logan's gaze followed it for a few seconds. Then he shrugged his shoulders, the previous tension seeming to slip from him, and wheeled her suitcase toward the house. "It's a little bigger than your house at the McG, but same kind of setup."

"I've come to realize everything at the Double H is bigger than at the McG. Even though I'd already looked up the ranch online, that info and pictures didn't prepare me for this. Your family owns a lot of land and a lot of cattle, don't they?"

"They do." He jingled the big H key chain at her. "These keys get you into this house, and they unlock most of the gates on the property, including the big one in the front."

She stood to the side as Logan unlocked the front door. Did his *Delta Force thing* make him somewhat of an outsider here? Something did. She could sense the strain between him and Hugh. She'd ask, but she didn't want him to bite her head off.

He pushed open the door and gestured her across the threshold. "Make yourself at home."

Lana took a deep breath. "A little musty, but nice."

"As long as the weather is cooperating—for today anyway—we can get a little fresh air in here." He walked around the room throwing open windows, the heels of his boots clattering on the hardwood floor. "This place has two bedrooms and two bathrooms, but one is the master, so I can wheel your bag into that room unless you want the other for some reason."

"You can leave my bags in the living room for now." She followed him down the hallway and poked her head into the first room, where a double bed and matching furniture presented a pretty picture. "Nice."

He disappeared through another doorway and called out, "This is the master. The bathroom's attached, so it's more convenient."

Lana stepped into the room behind him and touched the petals of a daffodil in a vase next to the bed. "This is a nice touch."

"That would be Angie, Hugh's wife." Logan's jawline hardened all out of proportion to Angie's welcoming gesture.

"Very kind of her." She pressed her fingertips against the mattress of the king-size bed. "I may have to move in here permanently."

Logan jerked his head toward her and he tripped to a stop.

"I—I'm just kidding."

"I know, but hey, if it works out."

"I think Charlotte might have something to say about that when she returns from maternity leave."

"*If* she returns."

"When should I make an appearance before the royal presence?"

"It's not like that." Logan smacked the doorjamb of the bedroom door.

"Okay, what's wrong?" Lana crossed her arms. He'd been a witness to all the drama at her home, and now she was in the same boat at his. "Ever since we landed, you've been on the edge—and I don't think it has anything to do with Major Denver or Gil's journal."

"I'm sorry." He shoved his hands in his pockets and hunched his shoulders. "It's not you, either."

"I didn't think it was."

"There's some tension between me and my family."

"Duh."

His lips twisted into a smile, giving her a glimpse of the Logan she'd come to know—and like—a lot.

"They have certain expectations of me, and I don't always fulfill those expectations."

"That's funny because there's tension between me and my family for the exact opposite reason. They have certain expectations of me—take care of Dad, send money to Mom, handle the situation with Gil... give up my baby, and I *always* fulfill them. Where has it gotten me? Trapped in a job in a place that I detest." She shook her finger at him. "So, whatever you do, don't give in."

"Come here."

Her mouth felt like cotton all of a sudden, but it never occurred to her to refuse his request. The look in his green eyes demanded her compliance.

She uprooted her feet from the polished floor and crossed the room to him, never breaking eye contact.

When she reached his realm, he pulled her against his chest, wrapping his arms around her. Her head fell naturally against his heart, thudding heavily beneath his chest.

He stroked her hair, and then he took her by the shoulders and gently pushed her away, looking into her face.

She blinked as if emerging from a sweet, sweet dream. "What was that for?"

"You looked like you needed a hug, and I know I sure as hell did."

"Anytime, Tex." Tilting her head, she touched her cheek to the back of his hand. "You ready to enter the lion's den now?"

"As long as you stick by my side."

"You've been by mine all this time. Where else would I be?"

His thumbs inched up the sides of her neck until he wedged one beneath her chin. He slanted his mouth across hers and caressed her lips with his.

When he drew away, he brushed his thumb against her throbbing lower lip. "Do I have to apologize for that?"

His voice, rough around the edges, had her parting her lips for another round. He didn't take the hint.

"No apology necessary. Did the hug not do the trick?"

"The hug worked. I just wanted more." He chucked her under the chin. "Call me greedy."

She'd call him whatever he wanted her to if he'd kiss her like that again.

"Ready?"

"Ready for what?"

He raised one eyebrow. "Ready to go to the house and meet my father."

"Oh, that."

"If you'd rather do it later, get settled first, that's fine, but he's not an ogre. Hugh made him sound like some hard taskmaster. He's not."

"I'm not afraid to meet your father, but give me a minute to brush my teeth and hair." She dragged her carry-on off the top of her suitcase and rushed into the bathroom, slamming the door behind her.

She met her own wild eyes in the mirror and whispered, "What the hell are you doing?"

Had she really come to Texas for her safety or because she wanted to be with Logan? Maybe both, and she should just admit it and stop beating herself up over it. She deserved to be attracted to a man, enjoy some flirtation—and kisses.

She brushed her hair back and secured it into a ponytail. Might as well at least look as if she were here to work.

When she returned to the other room, Logan was studying a painting over the fireplace.

Without turning around, he said, "This is the ranch. My mother painted it."

Lana strolled up behind him and peeked over his shoulder at the depiction of a blazing sunset over the Double H with a pack of wild horses in the distance. "It's beautiful. Does your mother paint professionally?"

"Just as a hobby. My father has always been Mom's job and always will be." He swung around. "We can walk over. Do you mind walking, or we can call for a car?"

"After that plane ride and the long car trip, I really need to stretch my legs."

The distance from her house to the family ranch was less than a quarter of a mile and the fresh air caressing her cheek rejuvenated her. As they drew closer to the house, it grew in size until she came face-to-face with a mansion. Who wouldn't want to be a part of this?

When they reached the front door of the white-columned house, Lana almost expected Logan to ring the doorbell but he grabbed the handle of one of the double doors and walked right in.

A woman poked her head into the foyer, and a smile broke out across her face. "Mr. Logan. It's so good to have you home."

"Thanks, Lupe. Nice to see you looking so well. This is Lana Moreno. She's taking Charlotte's place while she's on leave."

Lupe greeted Lana in Spanish and welcomed her to the ranch. "Do you want something to drink? Lunch? We're serving lunch later, but I can get you something now."

"Nothing for me, thanks." Lana stared past Lupe, taking in the curved staircase and the cathedral ceilings with the natural light pouring through a glass dome at the top.

"I'm good, Lupe. We just dropped by to see Junior. He wants to meet Lana."

"Of course he does." Lupe dropped her chin to her chest. "He still has to know everything that goes on at the ranch. It's good for him."

"Is he in his library or the great room?"

"The great room." Lupe's eyes flicked to the right as she licked her lips. "Nice to meet you, Lana."

"You, as well." Lana watched Lupe until she disappeared to the left. Then she pulled on Logan's sleeve. "Junior? You call your father Junior?"

"Everyone does." Logan shrugged. "His father was Hugo Hess, my father was Hugo Hess Junior, and Hugh is Hugo Hess the Third and likes to call himself Hugh. My family usually has to make things difficult."

Cupping her elbow, he pivoted to the right. "Great room is this way."

Their boots clattered on what had to be marble tile and Logan swung open another set of double doors that revealed a large room that certainly did deserve the title of great room.

A crystal chandelier cast a sparkling light on the

white-and-gold brocade furniture. A fire blazed in the grate of a fireplace that took up half the far wall, framed by a mantel of green marble flecked with gold, almost the color of Logan's eyes. The long, floor-to-ceiling arched windows afforded a peek outside where a covered patio with a bar and built-in barbecue stood at the edge of a sparkling blue pool with a waterfall.

Lana's gaze swept along all the exquisite material objects in the room to avoid looking at the humans—all eight of them, each pale face turned toward her and Logan.

Lana folded her hands in front of her to keep from grabbing Logan's arm, as she had a feeling that gesture would provoke these strangers staring at her, sizing her up—and she was just the help. She couldn't imagine the reception for Logan's girlfriend, even a pretend girlfriend.

Logan stiffened beside her. "Wow, what a welcoming committee. I thought I was bringing Lana over to meet Junior."

"I'm here." A man with salt-and-pepper hair above a rugged face lifted his hand and waved from his wheelchair.

Logan had failed to mention his father was wheelchair-bound.

"It's been a while since you've been home, Logan. What do you expect?" A beautiful woman with a perfectly coiffed blond bob extended her hand, her diamonds catching the light from the chandelier. "Now, come and say hello to your mother."

Logan stepped down into the room and strode toward the Hess matriarch. He took her proffered hand and leaned in to kiss her cheek. "Mother, this is Lana Moreno."

Lana, who'd been perched on that step almost held in thrall by the scene before her, jerked forward at Logan's words. Her boot heel hit the step on the way down and she stumbled a little, but thank heavens she didn't fall in front of this group.

She thrust her hand forward. "It's a pleasure to meet you, Mrs. Hess."

"Welcome aboard, Lana." She returned Lana's handshake with a surprising grip of her own. "You can call me Dolly."

Dolly and Junior?

"It's a nickname, dear."

Lana cursed her mobile face. "It...suits you."

Junior guffawed and ended up with a hacking cough. "I like her already, Logan."

Logan shuffled toward his father in the chair and shook his hand. "Junior, Lana Moreno."

"Nice to meet you, sir." Lana took his hand, his dry, papery skin hot against her palm. "And thank you for giving me the opportunity to work at the Double H. It's an incredible place."

"Beats those so-called cattle ranches out in California, doesn't it? You need to stick to growing lettuce out there and let us handle the beef." He winked and squeezed her hand tighter. "And what's with the sir and Mrs. Hess? Call me Junior. Everyone does, even my own children."

Logan turned to the rest of the people assembled and proceeded to introduce Lana to his brother Hugh's wife, Angie, his other brother, Cody, and his wife, Melissa, his sister, Alexa, and his father's valet, Carlton.

Lana felt like a bug under a microscope. Everyone had polite words and broad smiles, but they all seemed to be holding their breaths, as if expecting her to do something outlandish. Everyone except Alexa.

When she took Lana's hand, her blue eyes sparkled and danced, her voice hanging on the edge of laughter.

Lana could understand Logan's uneasiness with his family. They were weird. And why were they all here to meet her? Surely, they could've mobbed Logan after her meeting with Junior.

After the introductions, Logan asked his father, "Do you want this meeting with Lana? Explain her duties, the layout of the ranch?"

"Of course. I still run the place, don't I?" Junior's eyes flashed as they darted to his oldest son, Hugh. "Carlton, follow us to the library."

Junior put his motorized wheelchair in gear and Carlton hovered beside him as he zoomed from the great room through a door leading to another room.

Logan nodded to Lana to follow them. "I guess I'll see the rest of you at lunch. You can grill me then."

Despite the tense atmosphere among Logan's family, the interview with Junior went as expected. He asked her about her experience and training and warned her that the job might not be permanent if Charlotte decided to return.

At the end of the meeting, Logan offered to walk her back to the house. "Or I can drive you back in one of the vehicles."

She turned to him on the porch. "If you don't mind, I'd like to head back by myself. I want to unpack and get settled."

"I don't blame you for wanting to be alone after that reception in there."

"It was... Your father's nice. I like him." Logan didn't seem inclined to explain his family's odd behavior, anyway. She patted her thighs. "What happened to put Junior in that chair?"

"A horse."

"You're kidding." She clapped a hand over her mouth. "For someone like him, that must've been devastating."

"It wasn't one of ours." Logan squinted as he gazed out at the ranch. "A wild horse. The old fool tried to tame a wild stallion. Thinks he's still out there."

"The horse?"

"Crazy SOB." Logan squeezed her arm. "Let me know if you need anything. I'll be by later and we can get back to work on Gil's journal."

"Of course." She'd almost forgotten why she was here, had almost forgotten Gil for the first time since he died.

"Are you sure you don't want to take some food back with you? Angie got the house ready for you, but didn't put up any groceries."

"I'm not hungry. I'll do some grocery shopping later."

"See you later, then." Logan turned and hesitated at the front door as if gearing up to enter the gladiator ring.

Lana made it back to the house and put away her toiletries, leaving her suitcase unpacked in the living room for now. She didn't have to bother cleaning the spotless rooms and wondered if she had Lupe to thank for that.

She sat on the couch with her laptop on her knees and booted it up. As she started going through her emails, a knock on the door gave her a start. She blew out a breath.

She'd left all that behind her. The Double H represented safety and security. Logan represented safety and security.

Still she peeked through the peephole of the front door and wrinkled her nose at the sight of Logan's sister, Alexa, on her front porch, a covered tray in her hands.

Lana opened the door. "Hello."

"Hello." Alexa didn't wait for an invite. She squeezed past Lana into the house, holding the tray in front of her. "I thought you might like some lunch. Lupe's a great cook."

"Thank you. How thoughtful, but I told Logan I wasn't hungry."

Alexa marched forward, her blond ponytail swinging behind her. She placed the tray on the kitchen table and whipped off the cover. "Chicken enchiladas, rice, salad and a couple of sodas."

Lana sniffed the air. "It does smell good."

"Dig in." Alexa pushed the tray toward her and looked around the room. "I haven't been in this house for a while. It's cute."

"It's very nice."

Alexa plopped down in a chair and cupped her face with her hand as she planted her elbow on the table. "Are you really a horse trainer, here to work on the ranch?"

Lana sat across from Alexa and popped the tab on one of the sodas. "Do you want one?"

Alexa answered by grabbing the other soda. "Well?"

"Why else would I be here?" Did Alexa suspect something about her brother and what he was investigating? Logan had made it clear he didn't want his family in on his business—and Lana could see why.

Alexa didn't look like she could keep a secret if her life—or anyone else's—depended on it. And Lana's life depended on secrets right now.

"Is that why your whole family was eyeing me like some alien from another planet? I know it's not because I'm Latina because, well…you're in Texas."

"Oh, it's not that. Cody's wife is half Mexican." Alexa waved her fingers with their sparkly blue nails in the air. "We just thought you might be here under false pretenses."

"Why would I be? Why would Logan bring someone to the ranch under false pretenses?"

"Like if you were his girlfriend."

Lana's toes tingled at the thought, and she jabbed her fork into an enchilada. "No, but why would that be a big deal? I—I'm sure Logan has had girlfriends before and even brought them home—hasn't he?"

"Oh, yeah." Alexa took a gulp of soda from her can. "The last time Logan brought a girlfriend home, she turned out to be a gold digger."

Warmth washed over Lana's cheeks. "How did you know that?"

"She may have liked Logan, because who wouldn't? But she liked the family money more, and she tried to trap Logan into marriage."

"H-how did she do that?" Lana put down her fork and curled her fingers around her soda can.

"The oldest trick in the book, Lana. She got pregnant."

Chapter Eleven

Logan knocked on the door of the guesthouse, clenching his jaw. His little sister needed to mind her own business. She didn't run over here to bring Lana lunch out of the goodness of her own heart. Alexa didn't have much good in that organ pumping in her chest.

Lana opened the door, her cheeks flying red flags, her lips forming an O. "Logan."

He charged into the house, raking his hand through his hair and stopping in front of Alexa, who had half risen from her chair. "You need to zip your lip and worry about your own life, not mine."

"I was just getting to the good part." Alexa's lower lip protruded as she fell back into the chair.

"Out." Logan pointed his finger at the front door still standing open, Lana still hanging on to the door handle.

Alexa grabbed her can of soda. "Okay, but you're gonna thank me. Lana seems really nice and she's pretty hot. You have to learn to open up."

"And you need to learn to shut your trap. Out."

His sister jumped to her feet. "Oh, all right. I got

to the part where Violet told you she was pregnant. I didn't even get to the theft or the lies."

"Sorry to deprive you of all the juicy parts." He jerked his thumb toward the door.

When Alexa reached the door, she patted Lana on the arm. "You can thank me later."

Lana shut the door and then turned and leaned against it. "What is going on? Do you have a child?"

"No." He tapped on the kitchen table. "Come back and finish your lunch. At least Alexa had one good idea rattling in that empty head of hers."

Lana walked to the table and sat down, but she left the fork where she'd rested it against the side of the plate. "Are you going to tell me the rest of the story? And why did Alexa think she had to run over here and give me the lowdown?"

"Alexa obviously doesn't believe you're here as a horse trainer, but I'd rather have her think we have something between us than know the truth." He pulled out the chair across from Lana's, turned it around and straddled it. "Believing you and I have some kind of relationship, Alexa thinks it's her duty to fill you in on all the details of my life and to explain the family dynamics."

"Because she doesn't think you'd open up on your own?"

"That's part of it." He shrugged. "She's barely twenty-two. What can I say? I'm sorry if she embarrassed you."

"She didn't embarrass me, but I'm afraid she may

have embarrassed you. I know I wouldn't like someone else to be running around gabbing about my life."

"I'm used to it. That's why I knew as soon as Lupe told me Alexa had taken a tray of food to you, she had an ulterior motive." He scooted her plate in front of her. "Finish your lunch, and I'll tell you the whole crazy story."

As Lana dug her fork into the rice, he took a deep breath. He could do this. It had to have been a lot harder for Lana to reveal the truth about Carla, and his sister was right. He'd never get close to someone if he refused to share himself... And he wanted to get close to Lana.

"I was young and stupid."

"Weren't we all?"

A smile tugged at his lips and he gave in to it. "I met Violet in town—the small town a few miles from here. We passed it on the way. Her aunt lived there and Violet's parents had sent her out here to stay with her aunt."

Lana held up her fork. "Which should've been your first clue all was not well with Violet."

"Probably." Logan reached forward and dabbed at a string of cheese on Lana's chin. "We started dating, and long story short, it turned out she was more interested in the Double H than the LH—me."

"Like Alexa told me, Violet was probably interested in both—because who wouldn't like you?"

He cocked his head. "My little sister said that about me?"

"Scout's honor." Lana held up two fingers.

"How about that." He scratched the stubble on his jaw.

"How did you, and everyone else, figure out what Violet was really after?"

"She tried to force a marriage by claiming she was pregnant with my baby."

"I take it she wasn't, since you said you don't have any children—unless…" Lana pressed a hand to her heart.

"There was no baby, and then when it looked like her entire scheme was going to fall apart, she stole from my family."

"Violet turned out to be quite a piece of work. What did she take?"

"Knickknacks, expensive knickknacks, some of my mother's jewelry."

"Did you get everything back?"

"We got nothing back. She left our home and took off, probably returned to New York, before we realized anything was gone. Her aunt was mortified. I was mortified."

"Because you didn't see it?"

"Maybe I didn't want to see it. Violet was damaged. She needed rescuing. My family has never let me live it down. That's why I don't bring any women around. That's why they were sizing you up."

"Wanted to make sure I didn't steal the silver?" Lana's eyebrows shot up as she took a sip from her can.

"Something like that." He crossed his arms on the back of the chair and wedged his chin on top of them.

"I honestly think they believe I can't be trusted to choose my own wife or girlfriend, even."

"Ignore them." She shoved her plate toward him. "Do you want the rest?"

"No, thanks." He pushed off the chair and picked up the plate, still half full of food, and carried it into the kitchen. "I do ignore them. That's why I avoid coming home when I'm on leave. This time I had an excuse."

"I didn't mean avoid them completely. You can still come home but ignore their jabs."

Tilting his head back, he studied the ceiling. How much more should he reveal to Lana? Opening up to her might bring them closer together, but it also might make her dismiss him from her life forever.

He grabbed a roll of aluminum foil from a drawer and ripped off a piece. "It's not just the stuff that happened with Violet, it's the whole clan. My family members can't agree on anything. They're always arguing, complaining, putting each other down. It's exhausting to be around. You saw them on their best behavior."

"I'm used to tumultuous family situations. My dad's drinking caused a lot of chaos in our household with the older siblings taking off as soon as they could. I understand why you wouldn't want to be around that." She crushed her can with one hand. "Your family just has more expensive packaging than mine."

He held up the plate he'd covered with foil. "I'm

putting this in the fridge for you. You can have it for lunch tomorrow."

"Or dinner, unless someone can give me a lift into town to buy some groceries."

"I'll take you in for both—I'll buy you dinner and then take you to the grocery store."

"That would be great. In the meantime, should we get going on the journal again?"

"Absolutely." He walked past her, went back into the living room and picked up the folder he'd dropped on the table by the front door. "Printouts from my phone. That's why I came by—and to stop Alexa from airing my dirty laundry."

"Eh, that laundry was only slightly soiled. I'm actually kind of impressed by you." She tilted her head and her dark ponytail swung over her shoulder.

"Impressed because I'm a gullible idiot?" He smacked the folder against his knee.

"Because you have a good heart and a trusting nature. So many guys in your position don't. Always thinking the worst of everyone."

"I *did* have a trusting nature. That boy is long gone. Maybe that's why I haven't had a serious relationship in a while—at least that's what my nosy little sister thinks." Closing his eyes, he hid his warm face with the folder. "And here I am, rambling along like an idiot."

Lana grinned. "Women only pretend to like the strong, silent type. We'll take the strong, but give us a man who can open up a little."

"A *little*." He crossed the room and tossed the

folder on the table. "This has the photos I took of the pages in Gil's books—except that fifth one I didn't get to. I also have a notebook in there, so you can start re-creating your work."

"Can you help me?" She pulled out a chair and balanced one knee on the seat. "I was really just writing down the notes. I hadn't started connecting any dates or times or remembrances to the events. It helps to have them separate from the pages of the book and lined up one after the other."

"It's a good thing you only got that far. The thieves didn't get their hands on much that's useful." He took the seat next to the chair she'd pulled out. "I can help with that. Let's get started."

For the next few hours, he and Lana used the photographed pages from the books and copied Gil's notes onto pieces of paper for each book.

He didn't care what his family thought he was doing down here with the new trainer.

If they thought, like Alexa apparently did, that he and Lana had some kind of relationship going on, he could do a lot worse. Any man would be lucky to have a woman like Lana by his side. Did she share his enthusiasm for their... *Friendship*?

The electricity crackled between them. Neither of them could deny that, but she'd been skittish back in Greenvale. Since he'd put that down to her reluctance to showing interest in a man in front of the people who'd judge her for her past mistakes, he wondered if she'd be more receptive to his advances here.

He scratched out something he'd just written twice

and shook his head. They were on the verge of discovering the secrets of that embassy outpost and maybe the purpose of Major Denver's visit there, and he was plotting his seduction of Lana.

Trailing her fingers over his forearm, she asked, "Are you getting a cramp in your hand?"

"No, I'm good. Let's finish up."

She rewarded him with a smile that made his belly flip-flop.

He began writing again, with a little more energy. Decoding and seduction? One side of his mouth twitched into a smile.

He always had been a master at multitasking.

LANA DROPPED HER pen and flexed her fingers. "That's it. I'm done."

"And I'm almost there." Logan flipped over one of his pages and continued scribbling. "Next step for you is to fill in the columns to the right of the events with dates, times or any other number combinations you can think of. Numbers are usually at the heart of any code."

"Not now." She rolled her stiff shoulders. "My brain is fried after the flight, meeting your family, writing all these notes…my little heart-to-heart with Alexa."

"Don't remind me." His lips twisted. "Didn't I promise you dinner out and a grocery trip?"

"You sure did." She plucked her shirt away from her chest. "But I'm going to need a shower and a change of clothes."

"Nothing fancy. You saw the town when we drove through it, or maybe you blinked and missed it."

He stood up and stretched, and she allowed her gaze to flick across his long, lean frame. His story about trusting Violet and how she done him wrong only increased his standing with her.

She'd figured him as just about close to perfect, pitying her mistakes and her dysfunctional family. Seemed he had mistakes of his own in his past and a family just as dysfunctional as hers.

The fact that Violet had used a pregnancy to try to trap Logan into marriage made her stomach turn. She'd been accused of the same stunt when she'd gotten pregnant for real. Blaine's family had convinced him of that fact and had sent him off to his Ivy League college in record time. She'd never seen him again and he'd never tried to see the baby. And she'd accepted payment from his parents for never contacting Blaine again and giving up Carla.

Logan didn't need to know that part of her story.

She stacked their pages and waved them at Logan. "We're not making the same mistake twice. Is there someplace you can lock these up?"

"Not without raising eyebrows and alerting Junior that I'm trying to hide something. He controls all the safes in the house." Logan took a turn around the room and snapped his finger. "There are some loose floorboards near the fireplace."

"How do you know that and would anyone else know about them?"

"My brothers and I—mostly Hugh and Cody—

used this guesthouse as party central when we were teenagers." He crouched in front of the fireplace and flipped back the Native American rug on the hard-wood floor. "This space was big enough to hide a couple bottles of whiskey, a few packs of cigarettes and a supply of condoms. I think it can accommodate some pages from a notebook."

Clutching the papers to her chest she hovered over him as he tapped on the floor. Then he took a knife from his pocket and jimmied it between two floor-boards.

"Told ya." He lifted one floorboard and then tapped the underside of the one next to it and punched it out. He directed the light from his cell phone into the cavity and reached in with his hand. "There's something still in here."

"Some aged whiskey?"

He pulled out a blue box and pinched it between his fingers. "Aged condoms. I guess those boys didn't get as lucky as they'd hoped."

As he started to toss the box onto the fireplace, she put her hand on his arm. "Leave them. We should probably just keep everything the same so as not to raise suspicions."

Curling his fingers around the box, he said, "I don't think my brothers are going to come sneaking around to find a box of condoms they left here almost twenty years ago."

"Humor me."

"You got it." He held out his hand. "We'll put our pages in first and the box can anchor them."

She gave him their precious notes and he slipped them into the space. He dropped the condoms on top and replaced the floorboards.

He brushed his fingers together. "Nobody's going to find those...and nobody's going to be looking. You're safe here, Lana."

"What if they follow me here?" She pulled the rug back over the floor and smoothed it with her hand. "If the guys after me took the time to find out your name, it wouldn't be hard for them to trace us to the Double H, would it? They'd just have to do an internet search of your name like I did, and they'd find this place."

"That's if they find out my name."

"They're already in touch with Jaeger somehow. They could just ask him if they don't already know."

"Bruce or Dale would've mentioned my name to Jaeger? Because Jaeger and I never formally met."

"Believe me, Jaeger would find out the name of the man who brought him to his knees and humiliated him."

Logan cupped her elbow and rose to his feet, taking her with him. Placing his hands on her shoulders, he said, "Don't worry about that. This ranch is secure. My brother's not going to let anyone who doesn't belong here wander around the land."

"As long as you're nearby, I'll feel safe, Logan."

"I wish I could be closer, but talk about raised eyebrows. If I moved in here, my family would implode. Unless—" he touched her nose with the tip of his finger "—you want me to stay in the house with you. I don't give a damn what my family thinks at this point. If you'd feel safer with me…in the next bedroom, I'm there."

The thought of Logan sleeping in the same house, away from the prying eyes of people who knew her and her past sent a flood of excitement through her system, but it would blow their cover.

"If we do that, they'll know I'm here under false pretenses. They'll think you arranged to get your girlfriend a job at the family ranch."

"So?" He lifted his shoulders. "In fact, that's the way we should've played this. You're my girlfriend. I heard about Charlotte leaving and thought it would be a good gig for you."

"They'd probably believe you'd introduced another woman to the ranch ready and willing to take advantage of you and your family's money."

"Told you. I don't give a damn." He captured a lock of her hair and twirled it around his finger. "Should we revise our story?"

"Will your father fire me?"

"Are you a good trainer and teacher?"

"Damned good."

"Then no."

She placed her hands against his chest. "Let me think about it. It could be…awkward."

"It could be…fun."

She gave him a little shove. "I'm going to shower and change, and you're not my boyfriend yet so don't get any fresh ideas."

"Yes, ma'am. I mean no, ma'am." He grabbed

his jacket off the hook by the door. "When will you be ready?"

"Give me an hour."

"An hour?"

"If I'm going to be your girlfriend, I need to do you proud, Logan Hess."

He laughed but as he slipped out the front door, she could've sworn he whispered, "You already do."

THE HOSTESS AT the Longhorn Bar and Grill had given them a table in the corner, but they couldn't escape the noise and activity of the bustling restaurant. The locals didn't have much choice when it came to entertainment, so they flocked to the Longhorn with its Old West decor of red velvet wallpaper and brass fixtures.

Lana popped the last bite of her filet mignon into her mouth and savored its buttery smoothness as she raised her eyes to the ceiling. "I have to say the Double H produces some seriously yummy beef."

"Only the best, but you gotta give the Longhorn credit for their preparation." Logan narrowed his eyes as he gazed past her left shoulder. "Incoming."

Lana cranked her head over her shoulder and waved at Alexa, heading for their table.

"Hope you don't mind. When I told my sister we were coming here for dinner tonight, she asked if we'd join her at the bar for a drink, which means we'll probably have to put off the grocery shopping for tomorrow."

"I don't mind, and I can always eat those leftover enchiladas for breakfast."

When Alexa reached their table, she pulled over a chair from the recently vacated table next to them. She tapped the side of Lana's plate. "Did you have the filet? It's to die for, isn't it?"

"It was delicious. Have you eaten? Do you want to join us?"

Logan nudged her foot with the toe of his boot, but she ignored him.

"No, thanks. I ate at home." Alexa plucked a french fry from Lana's plate. "But I'm not above poaching steak fries."

Logan slapped her hand. "That's rude. If you want an order, I'll get Jeannie back over here."

Lana laughed at the interplay between the siblings. She'd had that familiar joking relationship with Gil. Logan could pretend all he wanted that he viewed Alexa as the annoying little sister, but the way his green eyes sparkled when he looked at her told a different story.

"Ouch." Alexa's big, blue eyes widened as she bit off the end of the fry. "It's just one."

"You're welcome to as many as you like." Lana scooted her plate toward Alexa.

"Well, maybe a couple more." Alexa stuck her tongue out at her brother.

"I thought we were meeting you for a drink, not dinner," Logan addressed Lana. "Now that she's over twenty-one, Alexa has been spending a lot of time in bars."

Alexa licked some salt from her fingers. "He's exaggerating, as usual. At least it's all legal. I never bought hooch and hid it in the guesthouse like you guys did."

"How do you know about that?"

"I have my ways." Alexa quirked her eyebrows up and down. "I do still want to meet you in the bar for a drink. I just came over here to see what's taking you so long—and to find out what you knew about Drew Halliday, the new ranch hand."

"A new employee? You're asking the wrong guy. You should be talking to Hugh."

"Yeah, well, I don't want Hugh to know I'm interested. You know how he gets."

"I know how *you* get. What's so special about this Drew Holiday?"

"Halliday." Alexa closed her eyes and patted her chest over her heart. "He's hot and he wears his jeans tight. What else is there to know…oh, and he's in the bar as we speak."

Lana raised her water glass. "Then what are you doing here?"

"Just wanted to get a little intel first, but it's obvious you don't know anything." Alexa snatched another french fry and waved it at Logan. "Hurry up."

As she sauntered back to the bar, Logan rolled his eyes. "I'm trying to get her interested in something other than cowboys in tight jeans, but Junior just keeps throwing money at her to do whatever she wants."

"I think a lot of twenty-two-year-old women are

interested in cowboys in tight jeans." Lana's gaze flicked over Logan's broad shoulders. A lot of twenty-seven-year-old women, too. "She'll figure out something."

"Dessert? Coffee?"

"No, I think I need to check out Drew Halliday and his tight jeans for myself." She winked at Logan.

As they made their way downstairs from the dining room to the bar, the noise level kicked up another few decibels. Country music blared from a jukebox and couples crowded the postage-stamp-sized dance floor.

Lana tugged on Logan's sleeve. "Alexa is over there, to the right, and it looks like she snagged her man."

"Oh, God. I hope he's not full of earnest questions about the ranch, trying to suck up. He's got the wrong Hess brother for that."

Logan put his hand on her back and steered her through the crowd to the bar.

Alexa jumped off her stool. "So glad you finally made it. Lana, this is my friend Becca, and this is Drew. He's new to the ranch, just like you."

Lana nodded to a vivacious blonde, who looked like she could be Alexa's sister, and to Drew, who tipped his black hat and returned the nod.

Since Logan and Becca already knew each other, Alexa introduced her brother to Drew and the two men shook hands, sizing each other up the way men did.

A few other workers from the Double H joined

the group and soon the drinks were flowing and the laughter bubbling. Lana had a couple beers, even though everyone kept buying rounds and the bottles lined the polished bar.

Logan clicked his longneck down on the bar with one hand and grabbed her arm with the other. "Let's dance."

Lana followed him willingly, ready to stumble through a line dance, but the music changed to a slow song when they hit the dance floor.

Without missing a beat, Logan swung her into his arms and propelled her across the floor with surprising ease and grace. Even though he'd revealed a few of his warts to her, the man was still pretty close to perfect.

He made her a better dancer or maybe just being in his arms felt like she was floating on a cloud.

Her head couldn't quite reach his shoulder, so she contented herself with resting her cheek against his chest, where his heart thudded beneath the soft material of his shirt.

When the song ended, her feet refused to budge. She could stay here forever, forget about everything and everyone—except Logan.

He leaned down and put his lips close to her ear. "You ready to join this mess?"

Her eyes flew open and she realized they were the only couple still clinging to each other as a line began to form across the room.

"I think I already wore out my dancing shoes."

"Me, too." He took her hand and led her back to

the bar. "I've worn out my bar shoes, too. It's been a long day for us. Are you ready to leave?"

"I am."

They said their goodbyes to the gang still yukking it up at the bar.

As Lana hugged Alexa, the younger woman whispered in her ear, "I hope you're more than just the riding instructor."

"Good night, Alexa, and good luck with your hot cowboy." Lana nodded toward Drew, who looked like he'd had a few too many.

On the ride back to the ranch, Logan asked, "What do you think of Yellowtail's nightlife?"

"At least everyone knows each other and there's no disagreements about where to go."

"You didn't see Mickey's down the street."

"We drove past it and I saw enough to know that's where the serious drinkers go. Don't forget. I grew up with one of those serious drinkers. Those dive bars all look alike."

"They sure do."

The movement of the truck and the two beers in her belly caused her to doze off, and she woke with a start when Logan stopped the truck to open the gates of the ranch.

When he got back in the truck, she yawned and said, "I'm sorry. I must've fallen asleep."

"Like I said before, we've had a long day." He glanced over as he took the turn toward the guesthouse. "You sure you don't want me to stay tonight?"

"I think I'll be fine. I'm on the ranch, I'll lock up,

the journal notes are hidden away…and you're just across that field."

"And you've got my number in your new phone. Don't be afraid to use it." He parked in front of the guesthouse.

Lana unsnapped her seat belt and slid from the truck.

Logan met her at the front door. "Tomorrow you can look at the horses and Charlotte's schedule, and then we'll do some more work on Gil's journal. Once you start matching some dates and numbers to the notations, I think we can send it off to someone who can make sense of it."

"We'll need to get someone interested first, won't we?"

"Let me worry about that. You just work on connecting some dates to those events that Gil painstakingly recorded."

She grabbed the front of Logan's jacket. "It's not going to be for nothing, is it? Gil's death?"

"It's not for nothing now, Lana." He brushed a thumb across her cheek. "Your brother died in the service of his country—however his superiors want to spin it. Nobody can take that away from him."

"Thanks."

He touched his lips to hers in the briefest of kisses. "Lock up behind you."

Once inside, she locked the door and the dead bolt. She stomped on the part of the floor that hid her notes and got ready for bed, barely able to keep her eyes open as she brushed her teeth.

After dragging a nightgown from her still-packed suitcase, she curled up in the fresh sheets of the bed and couldn't even indulge in her favorite fantasies as a heavy curtain of sleep descended on her.

Several minutes? Hours? Sometime later a man—Logan?—yanked back her bedcovers. "Hurry, Lana. You have to get out."

"Get out?" Lead weights lay heavy on her lids. She struggled to open her eyes.

"Come with me." Logan whipped back the covers on her bed, and she shivered.

"Hurry, Lana."

She tried to form some words with her fuzzy tongue. "Where? Why?"

"Fire! There's a fire."

She jerked her legs, but they didn't seem to move. She felt pinned to the bed, but now the acrid smell of smoke invaded her nostrils. "Fire."

"That's right. I'll save you."

Logan would save her. Logan always saved her.

He scooped her up in his strong arms and her head lolled against his shoulder, her nose pressed against his neck. She breathed in his scent, and her body stiffened.

Not Logan.

She arched her back or tried to, but the strange lethargy continued to claim her body. "Not…no."

"It's all right, Lana. You can come with me now." The man who wasn't Logan threw her over his shoulder, digging his gloved fingers into her backside through the thin material of her underwear.

She clawed at the man's back as he charged out of the house. The heat of the fire warmed her bare legs, which hung limply against the man's body.

She knew now that this man was abducting her and there wasn't a damned thing she or Logan could do about it.

Chapter Twelve

Logan cradled his cup of coffee in both hands on his second patrol of the ranch and sniffed the air. His nostrils twitched at the smell of fire.

He tossed the coffee that had been keeping his eyes open and placed the cup on top of the nearest post. A fire in the stables could spell disaster.

He tipped back his head and sniffed again. Then he didn't have to smell out the blaze. He spotted black smoke rising from the direction of the guesthouse—Lana's house. Adrenaline pumped through his system.

Taking a shortcut, he raced across the field between the ranch house and the guesthouse, shouting Lana's name and calling the alarm system for the ranch on the phone clutched in his hand.

Two seconds later, before he even reached the guesthouse, a loud alarm blared across the ranch and several lights illuminated the landscape.

When he could finally see the front of Lana's house, his heart dropped to the pit of his stomach as he made out a form collapsed in front of the house.

He charged forward and bent over Lana, her inert body splayed on the ground, her nightgown bunched around her waist and her panties pulled down on one side. What the hell had happened here?

He scooped her up, and she moaned. "It's okay. I have you now."

Her body went rigid in his arms, but she didn't move her arms or legs.

"Lana, are you all right? What happened? Can you breathe?"

Maybe the smoke had gotten to her. Clasping her against his chest, feeling her heart beat against his, he strode away from the burning house and laid her down in the field.

The alarm had done its job, and the fire crew for the ranch pulled up in a truck with a tank of water, ready to hose down the fire until the volunteer fire department from town arrived.

As he cradled Lana's head in his lap, she grabbed at his hand and opened her mouth.

He put his ear to her lips, but she couldn't seem to form any coherent words.

After a few attempts, she managed one word. "Journal."

"Don't worry about that now."

A tear leaked from the corner of her eye and she tried to form the word again.

Logan popped up and waved over one of the ranch hands. "Brian, sit here with Lana for a minute. I think she's suffering from smoke inhalation. I'll be right back."

"Sure, boss."

Logan rushed back to the house, flames crackling on one side of it, and headed for the front door.

One of the workers called out, "Logan, stay back. We don't know what's burning. There could be an explosion."

"I'll be in and out." He dived through the front door and whipped out his knife. The fire hadn't reached the living room yet, and he flipped back the rug and retrieved the journal notes. Thank God Lana hadn't thought about them on her way out—or she might not have made it out at all.

He stuffed the papers and the notebook inside his jacket and by the time he exited the house, the volunteer fire truck was rushing forward, lights and sirens on high alert.

He smacked Brian on the back. "Thanks, man. How's she doing?"

"Trying to talk, but I can't understand a word she's saying."

Logan took his place beside Lana and stroked her forehead. "Don't try to speak. Don't worry about anything. I got Gil's journal. Relax. A doctor's on the way and we can airlift you to a hospital in Fort Worth if we have to."

The news of Gil's journal seemed to soothe her and her head fell back in his lap.

His siblings in various stages of undress started converging on the scene, and Logan tucked his jacket tighter around Lana's body.

Hugh reached them first. "What the hell happened out here, Logan?"

"I'm not sure. I was outside, smelled the fire and then saw the smoke coming from the direction of the guesthouse. When I ran over here, I discovered the house on fire and Lana collapsed out front. She hasn't been able to say more than a word or two and seems like she's in shock or something because she can't move. I'm thinking maybe smoke inhalation."

"Doc Flanagan on the way?"

"Yeah."

"He can treat her at the house."

A few minutes later, Dr. Flanagan himself appeared and crouched beside Lana. "Does she have any burns?"

"None that I saw."

Logan lifted Lana onto the gurney himself. "Why is she so unresponsive?"

"It could be shock. Let's get her up to the house and I'll determine whether or not she needs to be hospitalized."

Logan rode in the back of the ambulance with Dr. Flanagan checking Lana's vitals while Logan held her hand. He should've insisted on staying with her tonight and damn the optics.

Forty minutes later, the doctor had finished his evaluation of Lana and she lay in one of the upstairs bedrooms, tucked under the covers, sleeping peacefully, her long lashes dark crescents on her cheeks.

Logan handed Dr. Flanagan his jacket. "You're sure she's okay?"

"Despite a low heart rate, all her vital signs are normal and her lungs sound good. Shock can affect people in different ways and lethargy is definitely one of those ways." He tucked his bag under his arm. "When Lana wakes up, and she will wake up, she should be fine. If she's not, you know where to find me, and if it's an emergency you know how to contact emergency services to have her airlifted to Fort Worth."

"Thanks, Doc." Logan shook his hand. "If you don't mind seeing yourself out, I'm going to stay with Lana."

"Good idea." Flanagan stopped at the door. "Do you know how that fire started?"

"I haven't heard anything yet. I'll talk to Hugh about it later."

When the doctor left, Logan got up and closed the door behind him. He settled into the chair he'd pulled up alongside the bed and watched Lana sleep, his own eyelids heavy.

When her cough jolted him awake, he sat up in the chair and glanced at the clock. Several hours had passed since the doctor left and daylight was seeping through a gap in the drapes.

Logan grabbed the plastic cup with the straw and hunched forward. "Lana? Are you awake?"

Her eyelids twitched and she raised her hand.

Logan grabbed it and squeezed—hard. "Lana? Are you okay? Are you coming back to me?"

Her tongue poked out from her mouth, and she licked her lips. "Thirsty."

"I have some water for you right here." He held the straw to her dry lips. "God, I'm happy to hear you say something."

Her lips puckered around the straw and she sucked up the water until she slurped it up from the bottom of the cup. "So thirsty."

"I'll get more." Logan lurched toward the bathroom and filled the cup up with cold tap water.

Lana drank most of that, too, before her eyes began to focus on his face and she struggled to sit up.

He bunched the pillow behind her to help. "How are you feeling?"

"I feel…okay. Kind of tired."

"Can you move your legs?"

"My legs?" She kicked one up under the covers. "Why? Did I fall from a horse?"

Logan ran his knuckles across his chin. She didn't remember. "There was a fire at the guesthouse. You don't remember?"

"A fire?" She ran her hands down both of her arms and pushed back the covers. Grabbing handfuls of the nightgown covering her thighs, she looked up. "Where's my nightgown? The one I was wearing?"

"Yours was dirty. That one belongs to Hugh's wife. The doctor was already here to see you and said you're fine, except for the shock—and now the memory loss, which he didn't mention was a possibility."

"Hold on." She held up a hand. "One thing at a time. Why was my nightgown dirty?"

"When I saw the fire, I discovered you outside on the ground, in the dirt. Then I carried you away from the house and put you down in the big field. So, yeah, your nightgown was pretty filthy by the time we got you to the house."

She nodded. "Okay. There was a doctor involved?"

"Dr. Flanagan. He's the local MD in town, but we can get you to the hospital in Fort Worth if you need it."

"I don't need any more medical treatment. I feel fine. I guess I escaped from the fire in time, before it did any damage." She gasped and clutched at his hand. "The house? Did it burn down the guesthouse? The notes on Gil's journal?"

"The house sustained some damage, but it's still standing and can be repaired. I have the journal notes from beneath the floorboards in my jacket." He tilted his head to the side. "You're the one who sent me back into the house to get them."

"I sent you back into a burning house and you went?" She coughed. "Are you crazy? Are you okay?"

"I'm fine—not crazy, either. It was important to you at the time."

"A fire." Lana sawed at her bottom lip with her teeth. "How'd it start?"

"I don't know yet." He circled his thumb on the back of her hand. "What are you thinking?"

"Why was there a fire just when I moved into the guesthouse?"

The twinge of uneasiness in his gut formed a solid knot. "I don't know, but I found you outside unharmed, and our notes on the journal were where we left them."

"But if you hadn't discovered the fire when you did, what would've happened? Would the guesthouse as well as the journal notes be ashes…along with me?"

He slipped off the chair onto the edge of the bed, taking both her hands and raising them to his lips. "Don't even say that. When I saw the house on fire and then saw you on the ground, a million horrible scenarios charged across my mind."

"How *did* you see the fire? Presumably you couldn't see it from your bedroom window, could you?"

"I was…on patrol."

She raised one eyebrow. "And that's something you do regularly when you're here at the Double H?"

"No. Only when there's something…or someone I'm looking out for at the guesthouse."

"So you *were* worried."

"Watchful."

"We need to find out how that fire started and where."

"I have a good idea of where. The back left side of the house was blazing—right next to the copse of trees, which were also on fire—outside the extra bedroom, the one next to yours. That's probably how you got out. You heard or smelled the fire and since it hadn't spread to the front of the house, you were able to make your escape through the front door."

"It's weird that I don't remember any of that."

"What *do* you remember?"

She wrinkled her nose and took another sip of her water. "I remember being incredibly tired. So tired,

I could barely brush my teeth. So tired, I was out as soon as my head hit the pillow."

"I was tired, too. Had to down a couple cups of java to stay awake. You don't remember smelling the fire or hearing it? You don't remember running from the house?"

"I remember—" she shook her head "—falling into a dead sleep."

"This amnesia you're experiencing is weird. I wish Dr. Flanagan had stuck around until you woke up. I'd like to ask him about it. I can understand the shock, but why can't you remember what happened?"

"I don't know, Logan."

The light tap on the door had him jumping to his feet and spinning around. "Who's there?"

Angie poked her head into the room. "Just checking on Lana. Is she okay?"

Lana cleared her throat. "Come in, Angie. I wanted to thank you for the nightgown."

"Glad to give it up. Yours was filthy—and don't worry. I'm the one who took the old one from you and got you into mine." She pushed the door wider to reveal Hugh carrying a tray of food. "We brought you some breakfast. Do you feel up to it?"

Lana squinted at the tray. "Maybe the juice and the tea. I woke up so thirsty."

Hugh stepped around his wife and handed off the tray to Logan. "Doc Flanagan said you hadn't suffered any injuries. We were relieved to hear that. Do you smoke, Lana?"

Logan jerked and the hot water from the teacup sloshed over the side. "Why are you asking her that?"

"Let her answer." Hugh narrowed his eyes. "Do you?"

"No. Now will you tell us why you're asking that question?" She took the glass of juice from Logan with just a small tremor to her hand.

"It looks like that's how the fire might've started—someone smoking near the tree line. A couple of cigarette butts were discovered."

Logan ran a hand through his hair. "Someone was smoking outside the guesthouse with Lana staying there?"

Lana's gaze met his over the rim of her glass, and her eyes flickered.

"Unless it was Lana herself."

Logan sliced a hand through the air, as a flash of heat scorched his chest. "She just told you she doesn't smoke, and I can verify that—as if I should have to."

"Hold your horses. I'm not accusing anyone of anything, little brother." Hugh winked at Lana. "What happened last night?"

"I—I don't remember." Lana wrapped her hands around the cup. "I fell asleep and the next thing I knew I was waking up here in this bed."

"You don't even remember the fire?" Hugh's eyes bugged out in exaggeration.

Angie elbowed him in the ribs. "She was probably in shock. I know I would be."

"Darlin', you'd be in shock if the nail lady ran out of your favorite polish."

Lana pursed her lips and her nostrils flared.

Logan should just let Lana give it to Hugh with both barrels, but that wouldn't help anything right now.

He stepped between Lana and his brother. "Hugh, you're an idiot, but I suppose Angie already knows that. If you're done accusing Lana now, you can leave. I'll talk to you about the fire later."

Angie ducked down and patted Lana's foot beneath the covers. "Hugh *is* an idiot, honey. Don't worry about anything he says. Just work on getting better."

"Yeah, since you were supposed to be taking a look at the horses today."

"Out." Angie shoved her husband from behind and closed the door behind them.

"That's just great. Your brother thinks I started the fire." She drained her juice. "What possible reason could I have for doing that?"

Logan hooked a thumb through his belt loop and studied the rug. "To wind up here."

"What?"

"I know my brother and I know the way his mind works, which is scary, but I'm sure he believes you started the fire and faked being in shock to make it to the house and this bed. Violet part two." He held up both hands as Lana opened her mouth. "I know. I know. I told you my family had issues."

She snapped her mouth shut and sniffed. "I really don't care what your family thinks—as long as you don't believe that."

"Me?" He smacked his chest. "You know what I believe?"

"The same thing that I do. The people who want Gil's journal or at least want to stop anyone else from getting it followed us here, got onto the ranch and set that fire to literally smoke me out."

"Damn it." He sank into the chair by the bed and stretched his legs in front of him. "That's exactly what I think, but I can't wrap my head around the how and the why of it."

"How? Jaeger got your name and passed it onto them. They did a search on you, saw your connection to the Double H and figured you'd bring me here for safety. We know the why—Gil's journal."

"It's not that simple. How would a stranger just waltz onto this ranch? Why set a fire? Are they trying to destroy the journal…or you?"

Lana pulled the covers up to her chin. "Maybe I'm in denial here, but if they…got rid of me, they'd have no way of decoding the books they stole from the McG Ranch. That wouldn't do them any good."

"Maybe they don't care about decoding Gil's journal. They want to get rid of it and the one person who *can* decode it."

"Thanks for bursting my bubble." Lana rubbed her arms. "But if they *did* set that fire last night, they had their best chance. You found me collapsed in front of the house. They could've finished me off before you came onto the scene. They didn't take that opportunity."

"You're right." Logan tapped the toes of his boots together. "They wanted to take you, not kill you."

"And you stopped them. They obviously didn't expect anyone to notice that fire until it was too late, but you did. You saved me, Logan."

"Thank God." He leaned forward and grabbed her hand. "If they had taken you…"

"Ouch." She drummed her fingers on the back of his hand. "You're crushing my bones."

He uncurled his fingers and turned her hand over. He kissed the center of her palm. "I'm sorry. Am I crazy feeling this way about you? Is it my imagination, my white knight complex, or do you feel something, too?"

"If you're crazy, I'm crazy, too." She cupped his chin with her hand. "Kinda crazy about you."

A stupid smile broke out on his face, and he relocated to the edge of the mattress. This time, he scooped her into his arms and planted a kiss on her mouth as if to seal some sort of pact between them.

She curled her arms around his neck and kissed him back, her soft lips moving beneath his.

He cupped her rounded breast beneath the gauzy material of Angie's nightgown, running his thumb across her peaked nipple and she arched her back.

Whispering against her lips, he said, "Is it too soon? Should I let you rest?"

"Soon?" She nibbled on his lower lip. "I've been waiting for this ever since I met you."

"One word, and you could've had me. I'm easy… when it comes to you, I'm easy." He slipped his hand beneath her nightgown and brushed his knuckles up her thigh and over the curve of her hip. "Angie took away your underwear, too."

"I thought at first you were the one who undressed me."

"I didn't want to take liberties." He slipped his hand beneath her bottom and caressed her silky flesh. "Like this."

She squirmed against him and raked her nails down his back. "The thought of you undressing me kind of turned me on."

"Everything about you turns me on." He cinched her wrist and pulled her hand down to his thigh. "Do you want to see how much?"

Dragging her hand across the erection bulging and aching beneath the rough denim of his jeans, she sighed. "Do you think those condoms under the floorboard are still good?"

"What happened between the opportunity we had to hook up at your house back at the McG and now?" His caresses stopped. "I'm not pushing you, am I? Taking advantage of your weakened state?"

"Everything changed. I feel like a different person away from Greenvale, a person not tied to my mistakes. I don't want to waste time anymore. Here we are closer to your departure, closer to getting a handle on Gil's journal, closer to maybe never seeing each other again."

"I can't imagine that, Lana, no matter what happens. Even if we never figure out Gil's code, even if

I never find out what Major Denver was doing in Nigeria, I have to see you again."

"Even with my baggage?"

"Carla isn't baggage."

"Everyone, including Carla's father, thought I had gotten pregnant on purpose to trap him—not so different from Violet."

"Except you didn't use the pregnancy to trap him. You gave him a free pass…oh, and you're not a thief."

"That's not what your family thinks." She plucked at the sheets. "Your brother thinks I set the fire to finagle my way into the house."

"I'm pretty sure I told you I don't give a damn what my family thinks. Only you."

"Then what I think is we should continue with our little make-out session because you've gotten me all hot and bothered."

"Yes, ma'am." He slipped both of his hands beneath the nightgown and ran his palms across her bare skin. He wedged two fingers between her legs and trailed them up her inner thigh.

She hissed between her teeth. "Tease." Then she dropped her head on his shoulder and pressed her face against his neck, baring her teeth against his flesh.

As his fingers crept closer to her sweet spot, she jerked her head back from his shoulder.

"Stop? Do you want me to stop?" He could hardly get the words past his tight throat and disappointment.

She crossed her arms over her chest and blurted out, "He tried to kidnap me."

Chapter Thirteen

Logan withdrew his hands from her body, making her feel cold and vulnerable all over again.

"Someone tried to kidnap you last night?"

She massaged her right temple, memories in bits and pieces assailing her brain. "The fire didn't wake me—a man did. He shook me awake out of a deep sleep, and it was only then that I smelled the smoke and heard the fire—otherwise, I would've never gotten out in time."

Logan had scooted back from her, his hands wedged against his thighs. "He was trying to rescue you."

"No! I mean, yes, I suppose he was trying to rescue me from the fire, but where is he now? Why didn't he stay?"

"Did he say anything to you?"

"Just some soothing words."

"Soothing words? That doesn't sound ominous."

"I thought at first he was you, but...but he didn't smell like you."

"Smell?" Logan's eyebrows jumped to his hairline. "What did he *look* like?"

"I don't know. I couldn't see."

"The smoke was that thick?"

Lana wrapped a hand around her throat. "I couldn't open my eyes. I couldn't move. Didn't you say that when you discovered me, I was paralyzed?"

"You had a hard time speaking. You couldn't seem to move your limbs." He hunched forward and grabbed a handful of the nightgown bunched around her legs. "Are you telling me you were experiencing that immobility *before* the fire? Before the panic and the shock?"

Lana nodded, as a cold fear whipped through her body. "I couldn't move. That's why he picked me up and carried me out. He threw me over his shoulder like a sack of corn."

Logan's jaw formed a hard line as he smoothed the soft material of Angie's nightgown across her thighs. "What happened? Why didn't he see his plan through? He must've just dropped you in the dirt."

"You raised the alarm. You saw the fire, which he wasn't expecting. He still had to get off the ranch lugging my lifeless body and must've thought he couldn't make it. So, he dropped me and took off." She fell back against the headboard, dragging a pillow into her lap. "Why couldn't I move, Logan? What did he do to me and when?"

"It must've been at the bar, Lana, and maybe he did it to both of us. I felt tired last night, too, but not to the extent that you did." He pushed up from the bed and paced to the window. "How many beers did you have last night?"

"Two. You?"

"I didn't even finish my first. I was driving home and these roads are dark. More than a few ranch hands have driven off the road at night after having a few too many at the Longhorn."

"You think someone slipped something in our beers? Who? Didn't you know everyone there?"

"Everyone except the new guy."

Lana covered her mouth. "Drew."

"I think I need to pay a visit to Alexa's hot cowboy. Is there anything you remember about the man who picked you up?"

Lana couldn't remember much except that he'd placed his gloved hands against her bottom as he'd carried her out—and that he didn't smell like Logan. "Not really. Maybe his cologne or soap. That's what brought back the memory for me. When my nose was pressed against your neck, I remembered doing the same thing to the man who carried me out of the house. That's when I knew he wasn't you."

"We can't have you running around the ranch sniffing everyone's neck—except mine. Do you think he's worried now that you can ID him?"

"But I can't, and he knows it. That's probably why he slipped me that drug. He knew its effects— temporary paralysis, even of the eyelids, and probably short-term memory loss. He knew I wouldn't be able to fight him or see him to identify him, and he probably set that fire so I'd go with him willingly."

"Even if you can't ID Drew as the man who picked you up, we can have a talk with him, but if we do he's gonna run and show his hand the minute he knows we're onto him."

"Maybe we shouldn't reveal that we know we're onto him." Lana chewed her bottom lip. "Unless he's gone already."

"I agree. Let this play out with him, and the best way is to go about our business today. Are you feeling up to checking out the stables? I'll come with you."

"Of course." She kicked the sheet off her legs. "I'm fine—now that the drug has worn off."

"I'll send someone to the house to get your clothes, if they haven't burned up in the fire."

"I never even unpacked, so if the fire didn't engulf the living room and my suitcase I should be okay."

"It didn't. Once your stuff gets here, you can shower, get dressed and come down to breakfast."

"Is this like a family breakfast where your siblings and in-laws are going to give me the third degree? If so, I'll make do with the food on the tray." She pressed a hand against her belly.

"You're in luck, buffet-style."

She blew out a breath. "That I can handle."

Pinching her toe, Logan said, "I'm beginning to think you can handle anything, Lana."

She gave him a weak smile. What she couldn't handle was saying goodbye to Logan Hess.

DRESSED IN A pair of faded jeans and a plaid work shirt, Lana crept down the curved staircase of the

Hess house as quietly as her cowboy boots would allow. She remembered seeing the dining room to the left of the staircase when they arrived yesterday, and she followed the sound of clinking silverware and the smell of bacon and coffee.

She peered into the room and let out a breath when Logan, sitting alone at the table, raised his coffee cup.

"Coffee?"

"Yes." As he began to rise, she put a hand on his shoulder. "I'll help myself."

After pouring herself a cup of coffee and loading her plate with pancakes and bacon, she pulled out the chair across from Logan. "Have you seen anyone this morning?"

"You just missed Cody and Melissa." He shoved the small pitcher of cream toward her. "How are you feeling?"

"Completely normal. You?"

"My brother is never normal." Alexa sashayed into the dining room, twisting her wet hair around one hand. "Heard about the fire. I'm glad you got out of there okay. Daddy says it was someone smoking on the property."

"We heard." Logan twisted his head around to watch his sister fill a plate with fruit. "Where were you last night when this was going on? I didn't see you outside. Did you sleep through the commotion?"

Alexa's mouth turned up in a smile as she plopped into the seat next to Lana's. "I was otherwise engaged."

Lana flashed Logan a quick look. "Were you with the hot cowboy?"

"I'll never tell." Alexa put a finger to her lips. "Do *you* kiss and tell, Lana? I noticed my brother never left your room all night."

Logan dropped his fork to his plate where it clattered. "You barely know the guy, Alexa. He's some temp ranch hand Hugh hired yesterday."

Alexa poured a stream of cream into her coffee and swirled it around with the tip of her finger. Then she popped her finger into her mouth. "Did I say I slept with Drew? Mind your own business."

"Ha, that's rich coming from you, who ran right over to Lana within minutes of her arrival to dish all my personal dirt."

"That's different." Alexa flicked her fingers in the air. "I'm a grown woman. I'll do what I want, when I want and with whomever I want."

"Just warning you—" Logan leveled a finger at his sister "—be careful."

Alexa spent the next half hour telling Lana about the horses and Charlotte's students.

When Lana finished eating, she picked up her empty plate. "What do I do with the dishes?"

"Lupe will clean up. We're the last ones to eat. I'll let her know we're done."

When Alexa left the dining room, Lana pulled up a chair next to Logan's. "If Alexa spent the night with Drew, he couldn't have set the fire and tried to kidnap me."

"My sister was acting coy. She never admitted to being with Drew last night. Sometimes she likes to pretend she's worldlier than she really is. Don't get me

wrong, she's not above bedding a guy she just met...
not that there's anything wrong with that."

Logan must've noticed her blush. After all, she'd
been ready to give up everything to him this morning and they hadn't known each other much longer
than Alexa and Drew.

"Maybe I can get the truth out of her—you know,
woman-to-woman."

"Give it a try. In the meantime, let's get you to
work and keep an eye on Drew and his behavior
today."

Fifteen minutes later, as Lana approached the stables with Logan by her side, the head groom sauntered out to greet them.

"Lana, this is Jake. Jake, Lana's going to be taking over lessons for Charlotte while she's on maternity leave."

"Good to have you on board, Lana. I heard about
the fire last night at the guesthouse. Are you all
right?"

"I'm fine, thanks." Lana clasped Jake's rough
hand. "Can you show me all the horses used for lessons?"

"I'll make the introductions and do you one better." He unhooked a clipboard from the side of the
stable door. "Here's a list of all our students and their
mounts with Charlotte's notes. Some students started
on one horse and moved to another. You'll see."

"Perfect." She took the clipboard from Jake and followed him into the stables, inhaling the scent of hay
and horse manure as whinnies and snorts greeted her.

She went down the line, allowing the horses to nuzzle her as she stroked their necks and fed them carrots, taking notes on the clipboard and listening to Jake's account of each mount.

About halfway through the introductions, Logan held up his phone. "Junior wants to talk to me at the house. Will you be okay?"

"I'm fine, Logan." Lana pushed at his back. "I'll catch up with you at lunch or something."

As Jake wrapped up the meet and greet with the horses, Alexa strolled up with Drew and Lana's heart flip-flopped. The man's easy smile didn't give away a thing.

"How do you like our little stable?" Alexa went right up to the horse called Ginger and kissed her nose.

"Little?" Lana rolled her eyes. "Hardly that. All the horses are beautiful."

"Some are a little feistier than others." She ran the heel of her hand between Ginger's eyes. "Like my little gem right here."

"Jake already told me Ginger is off-limits for the students."

"That's for sure. Ginger's all mine, but you can try Coco. She's a pretty little mare, spirited but not too frisky."

"Why don't you and Lana ride together?" Drew flashed a set of white teeth at Lana. "Alexa came out to ride, but I told her my break wasn't long enough and I didn't want to get in trouble my first day on the job."

The hair on the back of Lana's neck quivered. Could Drew be the man who'd set that fire and then carried her outside only to kidnap her? His voice gave away nothing.

"Maybe I will." Lana raised her eyebrows at Jake.

"I think that's a good idea, Lana. Alexa can show you the trails Charlotte uses for the more advanced riders." Jake hoisted one of the saddles from a hook on the wall of the stable. "I can saddle up Coco for you."

"I'd like that." Lana touched Alexa's arm. "Is that okay with you? Do you want the company?"

"If I can't have the company I expected, I guess yours will do."

"Thanks for that warm invitation." Lana curled her fingers around Alexa's arm. "Can I talk to you for a minute?"

"You girls go." Drew grabbed another saddle. "Jake and I will saddle the horses for you."

Alexa placed a hand on her hip. "Wouldn't want to cut into your break time."

"I've got just enough time for you, ma'am." Drew tipped his black cowboy hat.

As Lana propelled Alexa outside, she wondered if Drew was putting on a cowboy act to convince her he really belonged here. She couldn't exactly sniff his neck, but she could find out if he had an alibi.

Several steps away from the stable, Lana put her hands on Alexa's shoulders. "Girl, you need to be careful. Drew is as smooth as a baby's behind."

"He's so sexy though."

"Did you sleep with him last night?"

Alexa bobbed her head up and down. "I did. Don't hate me. We both had a little too much to drink and wound up in his bed. He took good care of me."

"Spare me the details." Lana held up her hands. "You stayed with him all night?"

"Sneaked back into my own bed this morning."

Lana's shoulders slumped. Drew couldn't have been the one who set that fire. Alexa had just given him an alibi.

She pinched Alexa's waist. "Just watch yourself. Don't fall so fast, so hard."

"Ha!" Alexa tossed her hair back. "That's almost funny coming from you."

The stable doors burst open and Jake came out leading Coco, while Drew had his hands full with Ginger.

Drew brought the horse to Alexa and helped her mount, his hands lingering on her rounded hip, although that girl clearly didn't need any assistance.

He patted the horse on the rump. "Watch out for this girl. She's as wild as someone else I know."

Lana rolled her eyes at Jake as he helped her into the saddle.

"Have a good ride, you two." Jake waved as they trotted off.

Alexa pointed out the paddocks Charlotte used for the beginners and, for all her flightiness, proved to be a useful source of information about the lessons and the current students.

Alexa gestured to the right. "There's a nice trail

this way with some trees and a river, which is cool in the summer. The other way has some rougher terrain, more rocky, fewer trees."

"Let's head to the river."

As they plodded side by side, Alexa asked, "Did you hear anything more about the fire?"

"No. I'm hoping Logan is finding out more about it now. I can't believe you slept through all the commotion, sirens and everything...or maybe you weren't sleeping."

Alexa giggled. "Oh, I was sleeping all right. I was so tired when we got back, I could hardly keep my eyes open."

"Really?" Lana drew up on Coco sharply.

"In fact, I'll let you in on a little secret that should make you and my brother feel better. Drew and I actually never made love. I was so out of it and he was the perfect gentleman. We did sleep together, but I really do mean sleep."

"You didn't wake up the rest of the night?"

"Slept right through the sirens and everything."

"And Drew?" They'd almost reached the river, but Lana's pounding heartbeat almost drowned out the sound of the running water.

"Sleeping right beside me all night."

"Well, as far as you know because you were sleeping soundly."

"Oh, I know." Alexa pressed a hand to her heart. "I felt his presence, and he was right beside me when I woke up and he insisted I head home."

"I'll bet he did."

"You think he did that to save his own skin?" Alexa leaned forward on Ginger and patted her neck. "He did it for me, for my reputation."

"Alexa, you barely know the guy."

But Logan's sister wasn't listening to her. She'd pulled out her cell phone and was reading a text message. "Oops, I have something to do back at the house. You can continue down this path and you'll run into the river. The trail follows the river for a bit and then opens up for a real gallop. That's what Charlotte does with her students."

"Alexa, about Drew…"

Alexa had turned her horse and waved behind her. "I know, I know."

As Alexa cantered away, Lana pulled out her own phone and sent off a quick text to Logan.

I think we have our man.

Drawn by the sound of the rushing water, Lana continued down the path to the river. Coco picked her way along the riverbank path until it veered to the right into an open field. Then Lana drove her heels into Coco's sides and the mare burst into a run.

As Lana's hair blew back from her face, Coco began to move erratically.

Lana leaned forward. "Shh, girl. It's all right."

Coco tossed her head and bucked.

Gasping, Lana gripped the reins and tried to regain control of the horse, but Coco had decided that Lana had overstayed her welcome.

Coco reared on her back legs, snorting and pawing the air with her front. As the horse came down with a jolt and charged toward the trees, Lana got the distinct impression Coco was going to attempt to dislodge her from her back—one way or another.

The next time Coco reared up, Lana slid from her back and landed on the ground with a thud that knocked the wind out of her.

Coco's hooves thundered past her, and Lana curled into a ball and rolled to the side. As she lay frozen, stunned, trying to get air into her lungs, she heard the sound of another set of hooves in the distance.

She rolled to her back and brushed the dirt from her face with the heel of her hand. She squinted at the rider approaching, his black hat bobbing as he galloped closer.

As Drew pulled up next to her and dismounted, he said, "Are you all right, Lana? Let me help you up."

Her mouth dry, Lana tried to scramble to her feet, still trying to suck in air. She croaked. "I'm fine. If you could ride out and get Coco for me, I'll take her back to the stables. I—I already called for help."

His gaze slid to her phone some distance away. "Really? With what? Smoke signals? I saw you take your unfortunate tumble, and you barely had a chance to catch your breath by the time I came to the rescue... again."

Lana blinked and tried to form her quivering lips into a smile. "Again?"

He stood next to her, blocking out the sun. "Let's cut to the chase, Lana. I have you alone at last…just where I want you."

Chapter Fourteen

Drew's low, smooth voice sent a chill up her spine. They were done playing games.

She spit the dirt out of her mouth. "What do you want?"

"You."

"Why? You stole Gil's notes. You know as much about what he wrote as I do." She rose to her knees and eyed Coco in the distance, relaxed and grazing.

"C'mon, Lana. We both know that's a lie. If anyone can decipher your brother's notes, it's you. We just want to find out what he was writing and who else saw it. You can help us with that."

"And once we find that out, we both want to turn his journal over to the proper authorities so we can find out what was going on at that outpost and why it was attacked…why my brother died. Isn't that right?"

"That's right, but your proper authorities—" he straightened his hat and pulled something out of his pocket "—may not be my proper authorities."

"Then once you use me, you're going to kill me. Why

should I cooperate with you at all? Who are you working with and why'd they attack the embassy outpost?"

He took a step closer, looming above her. "Because there are other people we can kill, people close to you, if you don't cooperate with us—and you don't need to know who we are."

She balled up a fist and pressed it under her rib cage. *Carla.* He must know about Carla.

"You'll never get close to her."

"I thought I'd never get close to you." He spread his arms. "And look what happened."

Her gaze tracked over his shoulder and the corner of her mouth twitched. "We're not as alone as you think."

Drew cranked his head over his shoulder and swore. In a flash, he mounted his horse and took off, calling back. "We're not done, Lana."

As Logan galloped toward her on his horse, Drew disappeared into the trees. At least after showing his face, he'd never be back on the Double H again.

Logan reined to a stop and jumped from his mount. "What the hell happened? Are you all right? If that rider went to get help, he took off in the wrong direction."

Lana released a little sob of relief. "That rider was Drew. Go after him, Logan. Stop him."

Logan rushed to her side and dropped to his knees beside her. "Did he hurt you?"

"He didn't have time. Never mind about me. Go after Drew."

"And leave you here by yourself? No way. He

could circle back while I'm out looking for him. He has a head start, anyway, and he's not going to be hanging around waiting for me to go get him. I don't know why he decided to show his face this time. He just ruined his plan to infiltrate the ranch."

"I'm afraid I'm not much of an actress. He knew I knew. I think he figured that out when he and Alexa came to the stables while I was still talking to Jake." She nodded toward Coco, oblivious to the turmoil she'd unleashed. "Wouldn't surprise me if he orchestrated my fall from Coco—or getting me alone. I had been riding with Alexa when she got a mysterious text calling her back to the house."

"Did he tell you what he wanted? At least it's not to kill you. He had that opportunity twice now, and failed to take it both times."

"They don't want to kill me...yet. They want my help deciphering Gil's notes. They want to know what he wrote as much as we do."

"Then the sooner we figure out Gil's code and get a professional to look at his notes, the better we can protect you."

"H-he mentioned harming others close to me. Do you think they'll go after Carla?"

Logan gathered her in his arms. "I don't think even Jaeger would give up that information to anyone. I think Bruce can keep Carla and the rest of his family safe...and I can keep you safe. Should've never let you out of my sight."

She pressed her lips against the side of his warm neck, feeling his pulse beneath her lips. "You always seem to save me just in time. I think Drew had a syringe in his hand—probably more of the same drug he gave us, and Alexa, last night."

"Alexa?"

"I got the details of her night with Drew on our ride together. She did go back to his place on the ranch with him, but she was so tired she fell asleep almost immediately. She *thinks* Drew slept with her all night, but he left her drugged and crept out to set the fire and kidnap me."

"Bastard." Logan curled his hands around her waist. "Can you get up? Are you injured?"

"I'm okay, and I think Coco's all right, too."

"Let's go find out."

When she was securely behind Logan on his mount, Coco's lead in her hand and her arms around his waist, she said, "At least Drew has shown his face. No more surprises from him."

"I noticed Alexa taking some selfies last night at the bar. Believe me, I'm gonna post his pretty-boy mug all over town, so he won't be able to step out for a cup of coffee."

"Alexa will be disappointed."

"She'll get over it when the next hot cowboy comes to the ranch."

Jake hustled out to meet them. "Logan, that new ranch hand, Drew, came out to the stables and saddled up Diablo without permission. I don't know what that boy was thinking because that right there is enough to get him fired once I tell Hugh."

"Drew misrepresented himself to get on the ranch

and get to Lana. He's a bad character, Jake. Spread the word on the ranch. I'm gonna call the sheriff in town so they can keep an eye out for him there, too. He won't be coming back to the ranch."

"And Diablo? That's one fine piece of horseflesh to lose."

"I doubt Drew is going to take Diablo anywhere. He'll probably turn her loose once he's off the ranch."

"You might want to give Coco some TLC, Jake. Looks like Drew put a burr or something beneath her saddle to make her bolt when I put her into a gallop. She tossed me."

Jake swore. "Are you all right, Lana?"

"I'm fine, but make sure Coco's okay. Poor baby."

Jake took Coco's reins and whispered in her ear, "Don't worry about that scoundrel, Logan. If he shows his face around here again, he's in for a whippin'."

"I trust you to handle him, Jake, but I think he's long gone." Logan put his arm around Lana. "Are you okay to walk back to the house, or should I drive over and pick you up?"

"I think the sooner I stretch out my muscles, the better. I'm feeling a little stiff and I don't want to cramp up."

"We need to alert everyone at the house, and I want to get one of Alexa's pictures of Drew printed off to circulate in the town."

"And I need to start assigning some dates and numbers to Gil's notes. I feel like we're racing against time now."

When they reached the ranch house, Logan told Hugh and the others about Drew. "Where's Alexa? She has a few pictures of him. I don't think he's gonna show his face around here again, but I want to give the sheriff a heads-up."

Angie said, "Last I saw her, she was headed for her friend Becca's."

"Can you do me a favor, Angie, and let her know about Drew? Maybe she knows something else about him that we don't."

"On it." Angie took out her phone.

Hugh shoved a hand in his pocket. "Are you gonna try to tell us that this Drew character is after Lana because she's a horse trainer?"

"I'm not gonna tell you anything, Hugh, but for now Lana has other business to worry about than Charlotte's classes."

However Logan felt about his family, he knew how to handle them and once again Lana felt an over-whelming sense of security in his presence.

He propelled her upstairs, leaving them to mull over the mystery.

When they got to the room she'd slept in the night before, Logan handed her the notebook. "You can't go back to the guesthouse, but I'm going to clear a space in my father's office for you to work."

"What about Junior?"

"Carlton has taken him into town for some physi-cal therapy. He'll be gone the rest of the afternoon."

"Let me change clothes and I'll be right down."

Ten minutes later, her face washed and dressed in

a clean pair of jeans and a blouse, Lana joined Logan in Junior's office.

He looked up from a cleared-off desk in the corner. "Are you ready to take a trip down memory lane?"

"Can you guarantee someone's going to look at these notes?"

"Once we get started, someone in a position of authority is going to want to read what Gil had to say about that outpost. Trust me."

She crossed the room to the desk and put her arms around Logan, resting her head against his broad back. "I trust you more than anything or anybody."

While Logan sat at his father's desk with his laptop, Lana started going through Gil's notes. Every family event he'd recorded in his books corresponded to a date—someone's birthday, someone's graduation, a school event. Lana recorded the month, date—when she could remember it—and year next to each event, starting with the first book.

After an hour's work, she had a page filled with numbers. "Logan, I have the numbers for one book. What now?"

"Let's see what we have." He swept his laptop from the desk and brought it to her. "I scanned all the pages onto my computer. Which book did you do? I'll bring up those pages."

"The first one you photographed." She dragged a chair next to hers and patted the seat. "Sit."

He double-clicked on the file that contained the scanned pages for the first book, the event she'd translated into a date, written in Gil's hand on the first page.

"I'm dizzy." She held a hand to her head. "What do we do with the numbers?"

"We start matching them to letters on this page." He placed the tip of his index finger under the first date and read aloud. "Two, sixteen, ninety."

"One of my older brothers broke his tooth on his tenth birthday. Gil and I weren't even born yet, but we heard the story a million times. February 16, 1990 was Hector's tenth birthday."

"Good job. Let's take a look." With a pencil, Logan skimmed through the printed out pages of the book, circling letters and words and then erasing the circles.

"What are you doing?" She peered at the pages, the words and notes all blurring.

"Trying to find his pattern—the two could represent every two words, the second word of every paragraph, the second sentence on the page, the second to the last word, and so on."

Lana slumped back in her seat. "We have to go through every date and every page like that? It could take all year—longer."

"*We* don't have to do it, but if we can just get verification that the dates represent some system for Gil, we can get experienced code breakers to go through the rest. It won't take them a year."

"Thank God. I knew Gil was bright, but I had no idea he could do all this."

Logan shoved his laptop out of his way. "You keep doing the dates, and I'll keep looking for the patterns."

She hunched over the next set of notes and put

her brain to work. She knew Gil meant this code for her because some of the dates only the two of them would know.

Occasionally, Logan's laptop would ding, indicating a new email. He'd glance at it and then go back to work.

After the fifth email notification, Lana pointed to the computer. "Do you want to turn that down or close out mail?"

"No. I sent a few email inquiries about getting this stuff decoded and I don't want to miss a reply."

They worked together for the next hour with the occasional dinging from the laptop until Logan pushed back from the desk and stretched. "I don't know about you, but I need some lunch and a little caffeine wouldn't hurt."

"I'm hungry, but I'm hungrier to get all these dates out of my head and onto paper."

"You keep working and I'll hit up Lupe in the kitchen and score us a couple of sandwiches and sodas. Keep an eye on that email."

"Deal." Lana rubbed her eyes. "Are you going to see if Alexa checked in yet? I'm a little worried about her."

"I'm sure she's fine. Angie said she went to town to visit her friend." Logan grabbed his phone. "I'll check, anyway."

He left the room and Lana continued recording the dates of the events. Each time an email came through, she glanced at it.

After several more minutes, she raised her arms

above her head and reached for the ceiling. They'd made real progress and she felt confident Logan would be able to crack Gil's code and have something to present to someone in authority. Then this nightmare would be over—and maybe she and Logan would have a chance to really get to know each other.

Logan's laptop rang again and she leaned over. Her pulse ticked up a notch when she saw a government email address. This could be something important.

She opened the email and read the first few lines. Her blood ran cold and she read the lines again, her head swimming, her heart pounding in her chest.

"Lunch is served." Logan backed into the room, carrying a tray of food. "Sandwiches, fruit, a bag of chips and a couple of sodas—the caffeinated kind."

He looked up and jerked to a stop, one of the cans of soda tipping over and falling off the tray. "Lana, what's wrong?"

When he'd entered the room, she'd jumped up from the chair, her adrenaline pumping through her body.

"You liar."

Logan's eyebrows collided over his nose. "What are you talking about? What's the matter?"

She jabbed her finger in the air toward his laptop. "I read the email. I know what you did, or rather what you *didn't* do."

"The email?" Logan gripped the tray, his knuckles white.

"The email that assured you that you and your Delta Force unit had done nothing wrong by not coming to the aid and defense of the embassy outpost in

Nigeria when it was under attack. That you'd done nothing wrong as my brother, his fellow marines and the outpost staff all died."

LOGAN'S HEART TWISTED in his chest as he took a step toward Lana. "I wanted to tell you. I wanted to explain…"

She charged past him and he dropped the tray on the floor and made a grab for her.

She spun around and held out her hands. "Don't touch me. Don't ever come near me again."

She ran from the room and he went after her, but stood helplessly in the foyer as she crashed through the front door. What could he do, restrain her against her will?

From the porch he watched as her figure grew smaller across the field. Was she going back to the guesthouse? Maybe she just needed time to cool off.

He could explain—explain that they'd been ordered to stand down. It had been another reason why he'd developed suspicions about the attack on the embassy compound, a reason he had to keep from Lana. She should understand. Gil was a marine. She had to understand.

He'd fix it. He'd get someone to decode Gil's journal.

His head hanging, he turned and went back into the house. The outburst had attracted a few members of his family, but the look on his face stopped them cold and they melted away.

He returned to Junior's office and dropped to his

knees to clean up the food, his appetite as AWOL as Lana.

Once he'd cleaned up, he cracked open a soda and collapsed into the chair at the desk where they'd been working. He read through the email that had set Lana off and then straightened up in his chair as he read the part she hadn't reached.

One of his superiors in the army had agreed to send his decoding request to the CIA. They'd done it. Once Gil's notes and Lana's dates landed in front of someone in authority, Lana would be safe. They'd have no reason to go after her.

He took another gulp of soda and dived back into Gil's mind—the mind of the man he couldn't save, the man he'd been ordered not to save—but now he could save that man's sister, whether she wanted him to or not.

The office door burst open and Logan jerked his head up. Had Lana seen reason already? Had she forgiven him?

His shoulders slumped as Angie, Hugh, Cody and Melissa charged into the room, practically tripping over each other.

Her face white, her dark eyes round, Angie said, "Have you heard from Alexa yet? We can't locate her."

A muscle ticked at the corner of Logan's mouth. Lana had told him to call Alexa, but he hadn't done it. "I thought you said she was with Becca."

"That's what she told us." Hugh's mouth had a grim twist. "But when Alexa wouldn't answer Angie's texts or calls, Angie called Becca. Becca's in Fort Worth, and she's not with Alexa."

Logan rose from his chair and flicked his tongue over his dry lips. "The Jeep. Have you tracked her Jeep?"

Cody answered. "She didn't take her Jeep. She left it at the guesthouse."

Angie glanced at the cell phone that dinged with a text message in her hand. "Maybe this is her."

"Is it?"

Logan took a step toward Angie, who looked up from her phone, her face even whiter than before.

"What's wrong, Angie? Is it Alexa?"

"It's Becca. Her conscience got the better of her— and she's admitting the truth. Alexa took off with Drew Halliday."

Chapter Fifteen

Lana swiped the tears from her cheek as she hopped behind the wheel of Alexa's Jeep, conveniently abandoned in front of the guesthouse. She felt for the keys in the ignition and cranked on the engine. Let Logan's family think he'd brought another thief into their bosom.

All the trust she'd invested in him. All her confidence in him. All a big lie.

How could he have kept that from her? She'd known about the other military units close enough to stage a rescue at the embassy outpost. She'd just never imagined Logan's unit had been among the cowards who'd refused to respond to the outpost's requests for assistance. Embassy staff slaughtered. Three marines slaughtered. Her brother slaughtered. And Logan biding his time in comfort and safety.

She stomped on the gas pedal and the Jeep lurched forward, taking her away from the Double H. Taking her away from Logan.

As she approached the entrance to the ranch, she slowed to a stop and jumped out to unlock the gate with her keys. Then she roared through, without closing the gate behind her.

She didn't even know where she was going. She couldn't drive the Jeep from Texas to Central California—that really would be theft and she was no thief. And no liar.

Maybe she'd hitch a ride to Fort Worth in town and trade in her airline ticket for a flight tomorrow. He could have her notes on the journal. He had a better chance of getting it decoded than she did, unless he'd been lying about that, too.

She couldn't work with him anymore, couldn't dishonor Gil like that.

As Lana tore down the road to the small town of Yellowtail, her phone buzzed in the cup holder. She was not ready to speak to Logan yet...maybe not ever. That's what she'd told him, anyway. She never wanted to see him again.

She slid her gaze toward the phone as it buzzed again and she sighed. He hadn't exactly lied to her. She'd never asked him point-blank if he'd been in a position to help Gil, but then why would she? He should've known that was information she'd want to hear.

She hadn't been completely truthful with him, either, allowing him to believe she gave up Carla purely from the selflessness in her heart, never mentioning the monetary reward she'd received from Blaine's parents for selling her baby girl.

She sniffed and grabbed the phone, at least to keep it from buzzing anymore.

Steadying her left hand on the steering wheel, she picked up the phone with her right and glanced at the text message coming through. She wrinkled her nose as Alexa's name popped up.

She hoped Alexa wasn't going to whine to her about Drew. She had to believe he was a bad guy.

She balanced the phone on the top of the steering wheel and read the message.

Please pick me up at Mickey's and don't bring Logan. Don't want to face anyone in my family and their I told you so's about Drew.

Lana let out a breath. Good. Alexa knew about Drew and it sounded as if she'd accepted the inevitable.

Lana swerved to the side of the road and texted back while idling on the shoulder.

You're in luck. On my way to Yellowtail in your Jeep and I'm alone.

She pulled back onto the blacktop and stepped on it. At least the Hess clan couldn't get her for grand theft auto now since she was delivering the car to its rightful owner.

Maybe she and Alexa could commiserate together.

When she hit town, she pulled into the parking lot behind Mickey's and parked. She scanned the half-empty lot and wondered how Alexa had gotten into town without her car or any of the Double H vehicles. Must've caught a ride with Becca.

Lana pulled open the back door of the dive bar and gagged at the scent of old beer and puke that permeated the hallway. Her father had lived for bars like this and her mother had sent her and Gil out to find him on many occasions.

She followed the hallway into the bar and squinted at the shapes huddled around the dim room. She bellied up to the bar and rapped her knuckles against the sticky Formica. "Hey, have you seen Alexa Hess?"

The bartender's nose above his limp mustache twitched. "I ain't seen her here today."

As Lana turned and surveyed the room, a drunk hanging on the bar sidled up to her.

"I seen Alexa, that cute little blonde."

"You have?" Lana tried not to jerk away from the smell of booze coming off the man in waves.

He tipped his head to the side. "Just went into the ladies.'"

"Thanks." Lana scurried from the room, not sure what kind of ladies' room this place would have, but anxious to get away from the drunks and the surly bartender.

She shoved open the bathroom door and stumbled into a small two-stall affair with a grimy sink stuck to the wall, a wavy mirror above it.

She banged on the door of the occupied stall. "Alexa? Are you in there? God, I hope you're in there and we can get out of this dump."

The lock clicked and the door swung inward but

instead of facing Logan's little sister, she stood nose-to-nose with Drew, as he stuck a gun in her ribs.

"Good idea, Lana. Let's get out of this dump."

She stiffened her spine. "Where's Alexa?"

"She's not hurt. I want you. I always wanted you, and getting my hands on Alexa and her phone was an opportunity I wasn't going to pass up. Where's your watchdog? The D-Boy?"

So, they'd always known who Logan was. Did they also know why he was so interested in Gil's journal?

"H-he's on his way. Of course, I called him when his sister texted me."

"Nice try." He flashed his boyish smile, but this time she noticed his yellow teeth. "You don't have any reason to be afraid of me, Lana. Instead of working with Hess to decode your brother's journal, you're going to work with us."

"Who's us?"

Someone rattled the handle from the outside and Drew wedged a shoulder against the door, preventing it from opening, and called out, "Occupied."

The woman on the other side of the door cussed him out but left.

"We're just another side, Lana. There are lots of sides in these conflicts—your side, our side, their side. What does it matter? Seems like your side is trying to keep you from finding out what happened to your brother."

"And your side is the one that killed him."

He shrugged. "Let's get out of here and get to work before that old harridan tries the door again."

Lana's brain whirred. Alexa's Jeep. She had Alexa's Jeep and the older Hess brothers had put a GPS tracker on the car to keep tabs on their wild sister. Would Logan even know to look for the Jeep? They all thought Alexa had gone to town with Becca. Why would they doubt that or go looking for her? And Drew would never drive around with her in Alexa's Jeep. Once he took her away in his car, Logan would never find her.

She had to stay as close as possible to that Jeep for as long as possible.

She covered her mouth. "I think I'm going to be sick."

Drew narrowed his eyes, and then dragged her into the stall with him. In this close proximity, she smelled his cologne or aftershave and wondered how she could've ever thought he was Logan—Logan whom she'd foolishly run away from.

He kicked shut the stall door and pushed her toward the dirty toilet. "Get it over with."

She crouched over the toilet seat, the putrid smells doing a good job of getting her to gag. She choked a few times and spit up in the water before he yanked her head back by her hair.

"That's enough. You're not sick."

As she staggered to her feet, she grabbed a bunch of toilet paper and dabbed her eyes and nose.

He opened the stall door and shoved her through, the weapon at her back.

When she stopped at the sink, he jabbed her with the butt of the gun. "What are you doing?"

"I want to rinse my mouth." She cranked on the faucet before he could jerk her away.

She cupped some water in her hand and slurped it from her palm. She swished it in her mouth and spit.

As she reached for another handful of water, Drew knocked the back of her head. "Enough. Do you really think one of these drunks in this joint is going to come to your rescue? I was able to pay off one of them with a twenty for telling you Alexa was in the bathroom."

With a shaky hand, Lana reached for the paper towel dispenser, realized it was empty and wiped her hand on her jeans.

Drew prodded her with the gun and she shuffled toward the door. He reached around her, opened it and stuck his head in the hallway. "All clear."

She could try to make a run for it, scream for help, make a commotion.

He pointed the gun at her back. "Make a move and you're dead."

He probably planned to kill her, anyway, once she'd helped with the decoding, but she still harbored a ridiculous hope that Logan would find her.

He had to. She hadn't had a chance to apologize to him yet. He must feel guilty enough for not coming to the aid of those marines. She knew deep down he had to follow orders, always knew that, just as Gil had to follow orders.

They hadn't had a chance to make love yet. It couldn't be the end for them.

"Move." Drew elbowed her between the shoulder blades and she almost collapsed from the force of his blow.

She grabbed on to the doorjamb. "Tell me what you did with Alexa, or I'll never help you."

"I'll show you a picture I took of her. She's tied up, but safe. But I'm not doing it here. My car's in the back."

She dragged her feet down the hallway, Drew urging her on with the gun at her back. When they stepped outside, Lana blinked. Even though the sun was setting and the clouds were rolling across the sky, it was still lighter outside than in the dreary bar where nobody could help her.

Drew grabbed her arm and marched her toward a black, nondescript sedan.

She dug her boot heels into the asphalt. "Wait."

"What now?"

"You want me to help you decode my brother's journal, don't you?"

"That's why we're both here in this godforsaken hick town."

"I have the notes in the Jeep. I've already started working on my brother's code."

"Hurry up." He pushed her toward Alexa's car and she frantically stabbed at the remote. What could she grab in there that might look like a sheaf of papers or notes?

As she opened the driver's-side door and buried her head inside, Drew hovered behind her and she could feel the gun by her right ear. One false move and he could blow out her brains. Even if they never decoded Gil's journal, they could be sure nobody else would, either.

Thank God, Alexa kept a bunch of junk in her car and Lana was able to gather some receipts and papers in her hand. She waved them as she popped out of the car. "Got 'em."

Drew scowled at the collection of trash in her hand, but didn't examine it too closely. A sheen of sweat had broken out across his forehead despite the chill in the air.

This was not his thing. He'd had help kidnapping Dale from a private home. Now he was exposed; they were exposed in the middle of a parking lot of a small town where everyone pretty much knew everyone else.

She stopped again and swung the keys from her hand. "What do you want me to do with the keys? Should I leave them in the ignition?"

"I don't give a damn what you do with them. I can't wait until I shut you up."

Lana froze, curling her fingers around the keys until they cut into her palm. "What does that mean? You're going to kill me, aren't you?"

"If I'd wanted to kill you, you'd be dead. We could've planted explosives in that house of yours on that other ranch. I could've slipped you something stronger in your beer last night or left you to die in the fire. They want you alive to work on this journal."

"What did you mean about shutting me up?"

He'd taken her arm and was propelling her toward the dark car. "I have a little something to relax you.

You didn't think I'd be driving along, holding you at gunpoint at the same time, did you?"

"I—I don't want to be drugged."

"Would you rather be dead?"

"You just said they want me alive."

"Alive, but dead rather than free to continue decoding the journal with Hess. Do you understand that, Lana?"

She swallowed. "Yes."

"Then let's get this over with." He unlocked the car with his remote. "Get in the passenger seat."

She opened the door and as she began to ease into the seat, she caught sight of Logan peeking around the corner of the building that housed the bar.

She almost cried out in relief, but sank to the passenger seat instead and stared out the front windshield. She needed to get out of Drew's line of fire to give Logan a chance.

Drew held the gun with his left hand, pointing it at her head, and fumbled in his pocket with his right. He pulled out a syringe and flicked the cap off with his thumb.

Lana smacked his hand with hers and the needle fell to the ground.

"Damn it, Lana. That's not going to stop anything. Now bend down and pick that up."

Gladly.

Lana twisted to the side and folded her body over, nearly touching her forehead to the ground.

That's all Logan needed. The shot exploded and

Drew pitched forward, his warm blood spraying her back.

She screamed and before the echo of it cleared, Logan had her by the arm and pulled her free of the car and Drew's dead body.

Hugh and Cody rushed forward and kicked the gun from Drew's hand, but they needn't have bothered.

Lana clung to Logan's shirt. "Alexa. He has Alexa somewhere, but he claimed she was safe and he has a picture of her."

Cody had rummaged through Drew's pockets and held up two phones. "This one is Alexa's."

Logan stroked Lana's hair and spoke to his brother over her head. "Look at the photos on Alexa's phone."

Cody smacked it against his hand. "It's password protected."

Hugh snorted. "You don't think I know her password?"

He rattled it off to Cody, who entered it and accessed Alexa's photos. "Here. He took her picture with her phone. Recognize the background?"

Hugh took the phone from his brother and blew up the image. "She's at the Yellowtail Lodge. Can't tell you which room number, but there aren't that many to search. I'll call the lodge right now, and I'll alert the deputies to head over there."

"Better call the sheriff, too." Logan jerked his thumb over his shoulder at the crowd of people forming at the corner of Mickey's.

Almost thirty minutes later after the questions and the medical examiner had arrived, Lana smoothed her hand against Logan's cheek. "I remembered Alexa's Jeep had a GPS tracker on it and I was stalling and just hoping to God that you'd know somehow I was in trouble, just like you always have from the minute I met you."

Logan kissed the top of her head. "Alexa's friend Becca called Angie to tell her Alexa never went with her but took off with Drew instead. Drew had gotten to Alexa before any of us could and someone had already seen the Jeep at the guesthouse, so when it was missing I figured you took it."

"It was such a stupid thing to do. Drew texted me from Alexa's phone posing as Alexa to lure me to Mickey's. I was still so fired up about…you, I didn't even stop to think about any danger, although it did occur to me that I could be charged with grand theft auto."

He hugged her even tighter. "I've never been so happy to introduce a car thief to the family in my life."

As much as Lana didn't want to leave the circle of warmth and safety, she stepped back from Logan. "I'm not sorry you killed Drew, but we're not out of the woods yet. He has accomplices. They'll be coming at me again."

"They're too late. In fact, all of Drew's efforts were a waste of time."

"Why is that?"

"That email you peeked at?"

"Yeah."

"If you'd stuck around to read the rest of it, you

would've found out that my contact at the CIA had passed our info onto someone in the code breaker division. And—" he tapped the phone in his pocket "—he just got back to me on the way over and told me it's a go. They want Gil's journal."

"We did it!"

She flung her arms around Logan again and as he started to bend his head for a kiss, a high-pitched scream drove them apart.

Lana twisted her head over her shoulder and squealed as Alexa broke away from a deputy and flew toward her and Logan.

She nearly knocked them both over. "I'm so sorry, Lana. I hope you're okay."

"I hope *you're* okay. You must've been terrified."

Logan nodded toward the sheriff coming his way. "Now you both better hope I'm okay because I have some questions to answer."

Lana caught his hand as he turned away. "You saved my life, Logan. I'll defend you to my dying day."

"I did it for you, Lana…you and Gil."

As Logan dropped his gun on the ground and kicked it toward the sheriff, Lana whispered, "I know you did. And now Gil knows it, too."

Epilogue

Lana folded her hands around the coffee cup and blew on the steaming liquid. "So, that secret shed at the embassy outpost contained weapons earmarked for a terrorist group?"

"That's what Gil discovered."

"And you think Major Denver knew about it and that's why he's being set up?"

"If Denver went out to Nigeria to visit that outpost and ask questions, he suspected something and probably got his answers. Maybe Gil helped him get those answers, which put both of them in danger." Logan pushed his half-eaten breakfast away.

"What does that mean, Logan? Who was using a U.S. Embassy to move weapons to terrorists and why?"

"Right now, everyone's pointing fingers at the assistant ambassador out there and his staff, who are all conveniently dead. During the attack that killed your brother, the weapons went missing. I don't know if they got into the intended hands or if they wound up somewhere else, but these are some serious accusations."

Lana set down her cup, the slight tremble in her hand sloshing the coffee over the side and into the saucer. "There's something going on at the deepest levels of the government and military, isn't there? Denver must've gotten too close to the truth."

"That's exactly what's going on, but the people who aren't involved, the people on the right side, are beginning to see the accusations against Denver for what they are—a sham."

"Then why doesn't the army drop the charges against him, bring him in?"

"Easier said than done. First of all, they're scared. They don't know who to trust...and then there's Denver himself." Logan scooted back his chair and stretched his legs in front of him. "He's not coming in until he's good and ready, until he accomplished what he set out to do from the beginning."

"Which is what?"

"Expose the people in the U.S. Government who have secret ties to terrorist groups in the region—and discover their ultimate goal."

"Foster unrest?"

"That's a given, but there has to be something more." He glanced over her shoulder and put a finger to his lips.

Alexa sailed into the dining room. "I know you two are trying to spend as much time as possible together before deployment, but you're teaching your first lessons this morning, Lana, and I promised to help you."

"And I am so grateful." Lana took a quick gulp of coffee. "I'm almost done. I'll meet you at the stables in about ten minutes."

"Ten minutes?" Alexa winked. "That's not nearly long enough."

Logan pointed at the door. "I'm here another five days. Don't rush me."

"If you insist—there is another new ranch hand I wanna check out."

"Be careful." Lana's voice shook. She still couldn't quite believe she was safe now.

"Don't worry. Becca's known him forever. He's completely vetted."

Logan mumbled under his breath. "Poor guy."

When Alexa flounced out of the room, Logan turned his chair to face Lana and patted his thigh. "She's right about something. Ten minutes isn't nearly long enough for what I want to do with you."

Lana landed in his lap and curled her arms around his neck. "We make a pretty good team, don't we, Tex?"

"We do." He ran his hands beneath her shirt and kissed her mouth. "Are you going to miss Carla?"

"I am, but I'm still going to visit her and you were right. Dale needs a chance to be her mother."

"You're as selfless as you are beautiful."

"About that…"

He put a finger against her lips, still throbbing

from his kiss. "Let's save some of our confessions for the next time we're together."

"I'll try not to judge you so harshly the next time. I know you were following orders. Gil would've done the same. He had his suspicions about the shed at the compound, but he stayed away as commanded." She tapped her fingers along his forearm. "I know you would've saved them if it had been up to you."

"I would've. You know, that's something Major Denver would've done and damn the torpedoes."

She smoothed a thumb between his eyebrows. "Denver is in a lot of trouble right now. I'd rather have you follow orders and come home safely to me."

"Home. You'll be here waiting for me when I get back?"

"Damn right, Tex."

"You think you're going to be okay on the Double H without me?"

She raised her eyes to the ceiling. "Well, there *are* plenty of hot cowboys on the ranch, and I'm sure Alexa would be more than happy to give me the 411 on each and every one."

He pinched her waist. "Then I'm just gonna have to make sure I leave you plenty of memories to keep you warm on a cold winter's night."

"Mmm." She wriggled in his lap. "Can we start now?"

"You have to teach your first lesson. Do you want to get fired already? I'm just the younger brother here. I don't have enough pull to save your job."

"I guess a kiss will have to do for now."

"I'll make it the most memorable kiss you ever had."

Lana's mouth curved into a smile beneath Logan's lips. She believed him. He'd come into her life just when she'd needed him most.

Maybe her little brother had been watching over her. She'd spent most of her life looking after him. Maybe he'd returned the favor by sending her a Delta Force cowboy to have, hold and love like crazy.

* * * * *

*Look for the next book in Carol Ericson's
Red, White and Built:
Delta Force Deliverance miniseries,*
Undercover Accomplice, *available next month.*

*And don't miss the connected books in
the Red, White and Built: Pumped Up series:*

Delta Force Defender
Delta Force Daddy
Delta Force Die Hard

Available now from Harlequin Intrigue!

COMING NEXT MONTH FROM

H HARLEQUIN®

INTRIGUE

Available November 19, 2019

#1893 SAFETY BREACH
Longview Ridge Ranch • by Delores Fossen
Former profiler Gemma Hanson is in witness protection, but she's still haunted by memories of the serial killer who tried to kill her last year. Her concerns skyrocket when Sheriff Kellan Slater tells her the murderer has learned her location and is coming to finish what he started.

#1894 UNDERCOVER ACCOMPLICE
Red, White and Built: Delta Force Deliverance
by Carol Ericson
When Delta Force soldier Hunter Mancini learns the group that kidnapped CIA operative Sue Chandler is now framing his team leader, he asks for her help. But could she be hiding something that would clear his boss?

#1895 AMBUSHED AT CHRISTMAS
Rushing Creek Crime Spree • by Barb Han
After a jogger resembling Detective Leah Cordon is murdered, rancher Deacon Kent approaches her, believing the attack is related to recent cattle mutilations. Can they find the killer before he corners Leah?

#1896 DANGEROUS CONDITIONS
Protectors at Heart • by Jenna Kernan
Former soldier Logan Lynch's first investigation as the constable of a small town leads him to microbiologist Paige Morris, whose boss was killed. Yet as they search for the murderer, Paige is forced to reveal a secret that shows the stakes couldn't be higher.

#1897 RULES IN DEFIANCE
Blackhawk Security • by Nichole Severn
Blackhawk Security investigator Elliot Dunham never expected his neighbor to show up bruised and covered in blood in the middle of the night. To protect Waylynn Hargraves, Elliot must defy the rules he's set for himself, because he knows he's all that stands between her and certain death.

#1898 HIDDEN TRUTH
Stealth • by Danica Winters
When undercover CIA agent Trevor Martin meets Sabrina Parker, the housekeeper at the ranch where he's lying low, he doesn't know she's an undercover FBI agent. After a murder on the property, the operatives must work together, but can they discover their hidden connection before it's too late?

YOU CAN FIND MORE INFORMATION ON UPCOMING HARLEQUIN® TITLES, FREE EXCERPTS AND MORE AT WWW.HARLEQUIN.COM.

HICNM1119

Get 4 FREE REWARDS!

We'll send you 2 FREE Books plus 2 FREE Mystery Gifts.

Harlequin Intrigue® books feature heroes and heroines that confront and survive danger while finding themselves irresistibly drawn to one another.

FREE
Value Over
$20

YES! Please send me 2 FREE Harlequin Intrigue® novels and my 2 FREE gifts (gifts are worth about $10 retail). After receiving them, if I don't wish to receive any more books, I can return the shipping statement marked "cancel." If I don't cancel, I will receive 6 brand-new novels every month and be billed just $4.99 each for the regular-print edition or $5.99 each for the larger-print edition in the U.S., or $5.74 each for the regular-print edition or $6.49 each for the larger-print edition in Canada. That's a savings of at least 12% off the cover price! It's quite a bargain! Shipping and handling is just 50¢ per book in the U.S. and $1.25 per book in Canada.* I understand that accepting the 2 free books and gifts places me under no obligation to buy anything. I can always return a shipment and cancel at any time. The free books and gifts are mine to keep no matter what I decide.

Choose one: ☐ **Harlequin Intrigue®**
Regular-Print
(182/382 HDN GNXC)

☐ **Harlequin Intrigue®**
Larger-Print
(199/399 HDN GNXC)

Name (please print)

Address   Apt. #

City   State/Province   Zip/Postal Code

Mail to the Reader Service:
IN U.S.A.: P.O. Box 1341, Buffalo, NY 14240-8531
IN CANADA: P.O. Box 603, Fort Erie, Ontario L2A 5X3

Want to try 2 free books from another series? Call 1-800-873-8635 or visit www.ReaderService.com.

---

*Terms and prices subject to change without notice. Prices do not include sales taxes, which will be charged (if applicable) based on your state or country of residence. Canadian residents will be charged applicable taxes. Offer not valid in Quebec. This offer is limited to one order per household. Books received may not be as shown. Not valid for current subscribers to Harlequin Intrigue books. All orders subject to approval. Credit or debit balances in a customer's account(s) may be offset by any other outstanding balance owed by or to the customer. Please allow 4 to 6 weeks for delivery. Offer available while quantities last.

Your Privacy—The Reader Service is committed to protecting your privacy. Our Privacy Policy is available online at www.ReaderService.com or upon request from the Reader Service. We make a portion of our mailing list available to reputable third parties that offer products we believe may interest you. If you prefer that we not exchange your name with third parties, or if you wish to clarify or modify your communication preferences, please visit us at www.ReaderService.com/consumerschoice or write to us at Reader Service Preference Service, P.O. Box 9062, Buffalo, NY 14240-9062. Include your complete name and address.

HI20

SPECIAL EXCERPT FROM

H HARLEQUIN®

INTRIGUE

When her WITSEC location is compromised,
former profiler Gemma Hanson turns to the only man
who can keep her safe: Sheriff Kellan Slater. The only
problem is, they share a complicated past...and an
intense chemistry that has never cooled.

Read on for a sneak peek of
Safety Breach,
part of Longview Ridge Ranch
by USA TODAY bestselling author Delores Fossen.

"Why did you say you owed me?" she asked.

The question came out of the blue and threw him, so
much so that he gulped down too much coffee and nearly
choked. Hardly the reaction for a tough-nosed cop. But
his reaction to her hadn't exactly been all badge, either.

Kellan lifted his shoulder and wanted to kick himself
for ever bringing it up in the first place. Bad timing, he
thought, and wondered if there would ever be a good time
for him to grovel.

"I didn't stop Eric from shooting you that night." He
said that fast. Not a drop of sugarcoating. "You, my father
and Dusty. I'm sorry for that."

Her silence and the shimmering look in her eyes made
him stupid, and that was the only excuse he could come
up with for why he kept talking.

"It's easier for me to toss some of the blame at you for not ID'ing a killer sooner," he added. And he still did blame her, in part, for that. "But it was my job to stop him before he killed two people and injured another while he was right under my nose."

The silence just kept on going. So much so that Kellan turned, ready to go back to his desk so that he wouldn't continue to prattle on. Gemma stopped him by putting her hand on his arm. It was like a trigger that sent his gaze searching for hers. Wasn't hard to find when she stood and met him eye to eye.

"It was easier for me to toss some of the blame at you, too." She made another of those sighs. "But there was no stopping Eric that night. The stopping should have happened prior to that. I should have seen the signs." When he started to speak, Gemma lifted her hand to silence him. "And please don't tell me that it's all right, that I'm not at fault. I don't think I could take that right now."

Unfortunately, Kellan understood just what she meant. They were both still hurting, and a mutual sympathyfest was only going to make it harder. They couldn't go back. Couldn't undo. And that left them with only one direction. Looking ahead and putting this son of a bitch in a hole where he belonged.

Don't miss Safety Breach *by Delores Fossen,
available December 2019 wherever
Harlequin® Intrigue books and ebooks are sold.*

Harlequin.com

Copyright © 2019 by Delores Fossen

HSEEXP50496

**Don't miss this holiday Western romance
from *USA TODAY* bestselling author**

DELORES FOSSEN

**Sometimes a little Christmas magic can
rekindle the most unexpected romances...**

"Fossen creates sexy cowboys and fast-moving plots that will take
your breath away." —Lori Wilde, *New York Times* bestselling author

Order your copy today!

HQNBooks.com

PHDFCWC1119

Need an adrenaline rush from nail-biting tales
(and irresistible males)?

Check out **Harlequin Intrigue**®
and **Harlequin**® **Romantic Suspense** books!

New books available every month!

CONNECT WITH US AT:

Facebook.com/groups/HarlequinConnection

 Facebook.com/HarlequinBooks

Twitter.com/HarlequinBooks

 Instagram.com/HarlequinBooks

Pinterest.com/HarlequinBooks

ReaderService.com

**ROMANCE WHEN
YOU NEED IT**

SGENRE2018

Looking for more satisfying love stories
with community and family at their core?

Check out **Harlequin®** Special Edition
and **Love Inspired®** books!

New books available every month!

CONNECT WITH US AT:

Facebook.com/groups/HarlequinConnection

 Facebook.com/HarlequinBooks

Twitter.com/HarlequinBooks

Instagram.com/HarlequinBooks

Pinterest.com/HarlequinBooks

ReaderService.com

**ROMANCE WHEN
YOU NEED IT**

HFGENRE2018

Love Harlequin romance?

DISCOVER.

Be the first to find out about promotions,
news and exclusive content!

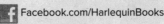

Facebook.com/HarlequinBooks

Twitter.com/HarlequinBooks

Instagram.com/HarlequinBooks

Pinterest.com/HarlequinBooks

ReaderService.com

EXPLORE.

Sign up for the Harlequin e-newsletter and
download a free book from any series at
TryHarlequin.com.

CONNECT.

Join our Harlequin community to share
your thoughts and connect with other
romance readers!
Facebook.com/groups/HarlequinConnection

HARLEQUIN®

**ROMANCE WHEN
YOU NEED IT**

HSOCIAL2018